STONE ARCH BOOKS
a capstone imprint

THE BATMAN STRIKES!®

STONE ARCH BOOKS™

Published in 2015 by Stone Arch Books
A Capstone Imprint
1710 Roe Crest Drive
North Mankato, MN 56003
www.capstonepub.com

Originally published by DC Comics in the U.S. in single magazine form as The Batman Strikes! #9.

DC Comics
1700 Broadway, New York, NY 10019
A Warner Bros. Entertainment Company

Printed in China by Nordica.
0914/CA21401510
092014 008470NOROS15

Cataloging-in-Publication Data is available at the Library of Congress website.
ISBN: 978-1-4342-9743-3 (library binding)

Summary: Why is the Joker now claiming he's sane? It's up to Batman to figure out this mad mystery before the Clown Prince of Crime is free of Arkham Asylum . . . forever.

STONE ARCH BOOKS
Ashley C. Andersen Zantop *Publisher*
Michael Dahl *Editorial Director*
Eliza Leahy *Editor*
Heather Kindseth *Creative Director*
Peggie Carley *Designer*
Tori Abraham *Production Specialist*

DC COMICS
Nachie Castro *Original U.S. Editor*

SANITY PLEA!

BILL MATHENY ....WRITER
CHRISTOPHER JONES ....PENCILLER
TERRY BEATTY...INKER
HEROIC AGE...COLORIST
PAT BROSSEAU ....LETTERER

BATMAN CREATED BY BOB KANE

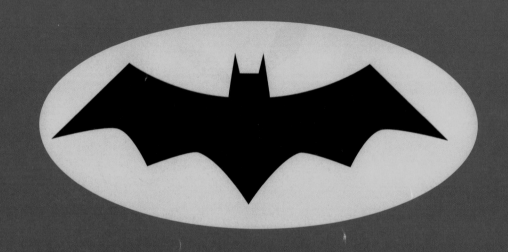

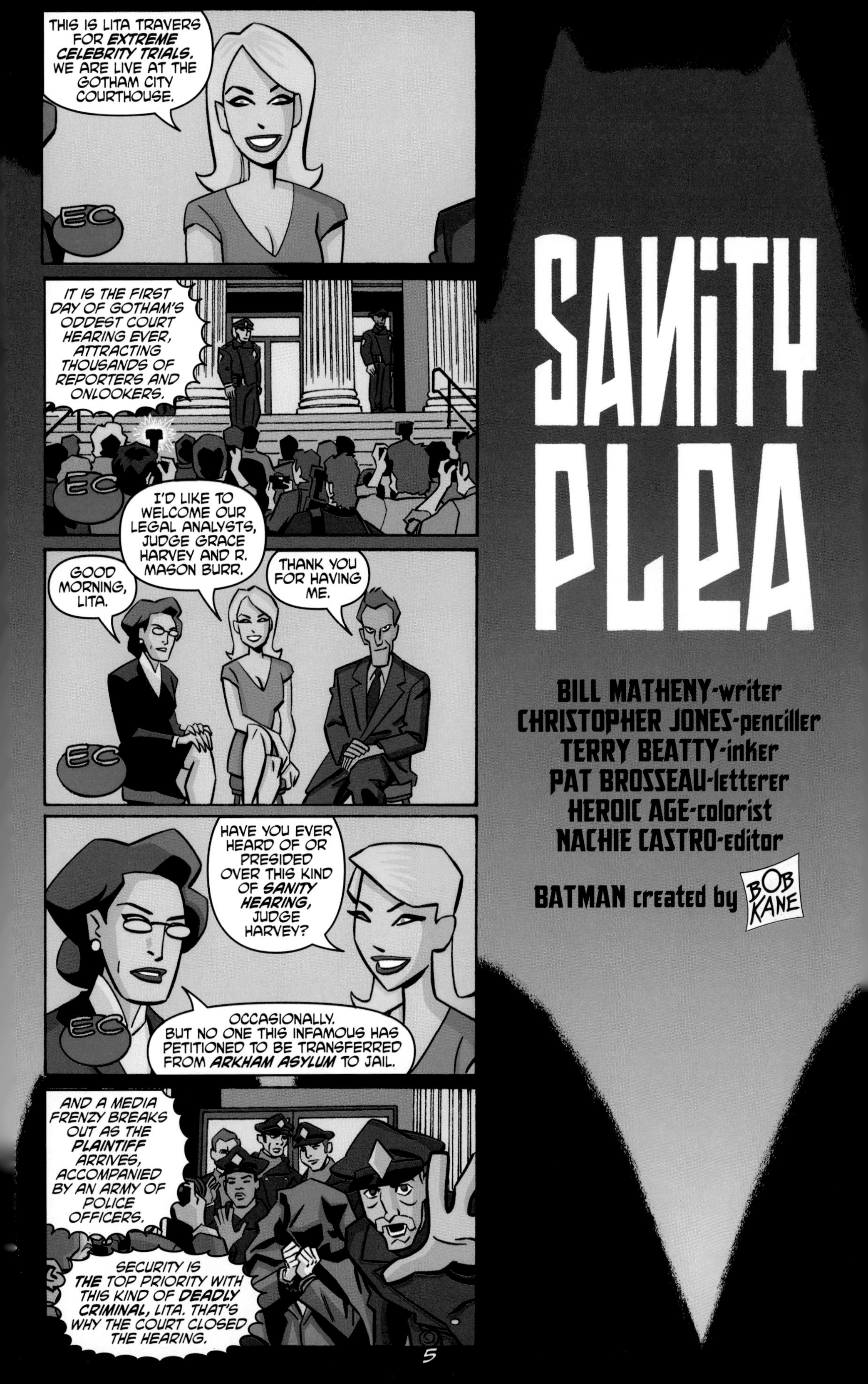
THIS IS LITA TRAVERS FOR EXTREME CELEBRITY TRIALS. WE ARE LIVE AT THE GOTHAM CITY COURTHOUSE.
EC
SANITY PLEA
BILL MATHENY-writer
CHRISTOPHER JONES-penciller
TERRY BEATTY-inker
PAT BROSSEAU-letterer
HEROIC AGE-colorist
NACHIE CASTRO-editor
BATMAN created by BOB KANE
IT IS THE FIRST DAY OF GOTHAM'S ODDEST COURT HEARING EVER, ATTRACTING THOUSANDS OF REPORTERS AND ONLOOKERS.
EC
I'D LIKE TO WELCOME OUR LEGAL ANALYSTS, JUDGE GRACE HARVEY AND R. MASON BURR.
GOOD MORNING, LITA.
THANK YOU FOR HAVING ME.
EC
HAVE YOU EVER HEARD OF OR PRESIDED OVER THIS KIND OF SANITY HEARING, JUDGE HARVEY?
EC
OCCASIONALLY. BUT NO ONE THIS INFAMOUS HAS PETITIONED TO BE TRANSFERRED FROM ARKHAM ASYLUM TO JAIL.
AND A MEDIA FRENZY BREAKS OUT AS THE PLAINTIFF ARRIVES, ACCOMPANIED BY AN ARMY OF POLICE OFFICERS.
SECURITY IS THE TOP PRIORITY WITH THIS KIND OF DEADLY CRIMINAL, LITA. THAT'S WHY THE COURT CLOSED THE HEARING.

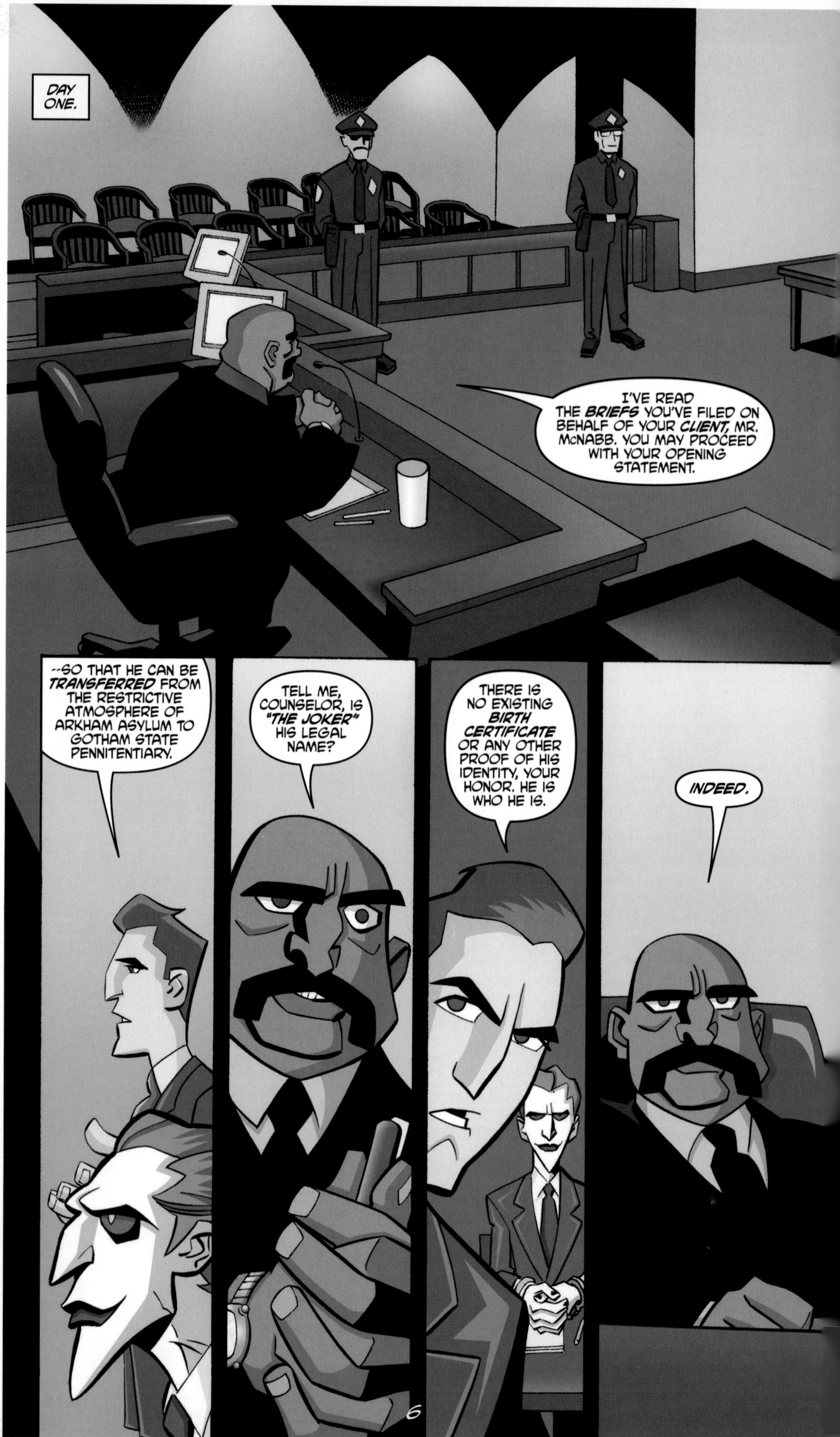
DAY ONE.
I'VE READ THE BRIEFS YOU'VE FILED ON BEHALF OF YOUR CLIENT, MR. McNABB. YOU MAY PROCEED WITH YOUR OPENING STATEMENT.
--SO THAT HE CAN BE TRANSFERRED FROM THE RESTRICTIVE ATMOSPHERE OF ARKHAM ASYLUM TO GOTHAM STATE PENNITENTIARY.
TELL ME, COUNSELOR, IS "THE JOKER" HIS LEGAL NAME?
THERE IS NO EXISTING BIRTH CERTIFICATE OR ANY OTHER PROOF OF HIS IDENTITY, YOUR HONOR. HE IS WHO HE IS.
INDEED.

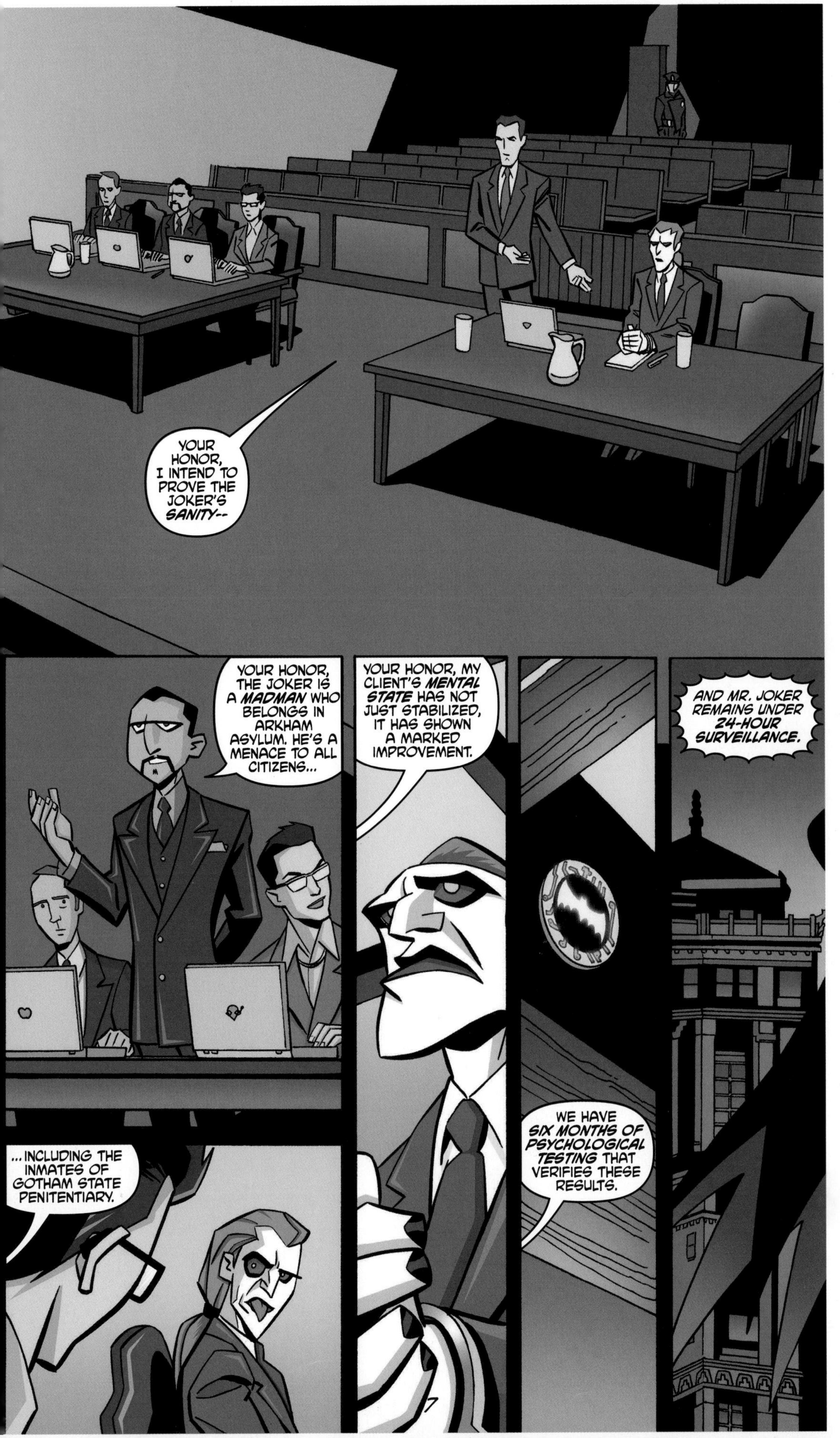
YOUR HONOR, I INTEND TO PROVE THE JOKER'S SANITY--
YOUR HONOR, THE JOKER IS A MADMAN WHO BELONGS IN ARKHAM ASYLUM. HE'S A MENACE TO ALL CITIZENS...
...INCLUDING THE INMATES OF GOTHAM STATE PENITENTIARY.
YOUR HONOR, MY CLIENT'S MENTAL STATE HAS NOT JUST STABILIZED, IT HAS SHOWN A MARKED IMPROVEMENT.
WE HAVE SIX MONTHS OF PSYCHOLOGICAL TESTING THAT VERIFIES THESE RESULTS.
AND MR. JOKER REMAINS UNDER 24-HOUR SURVEILLANCE.

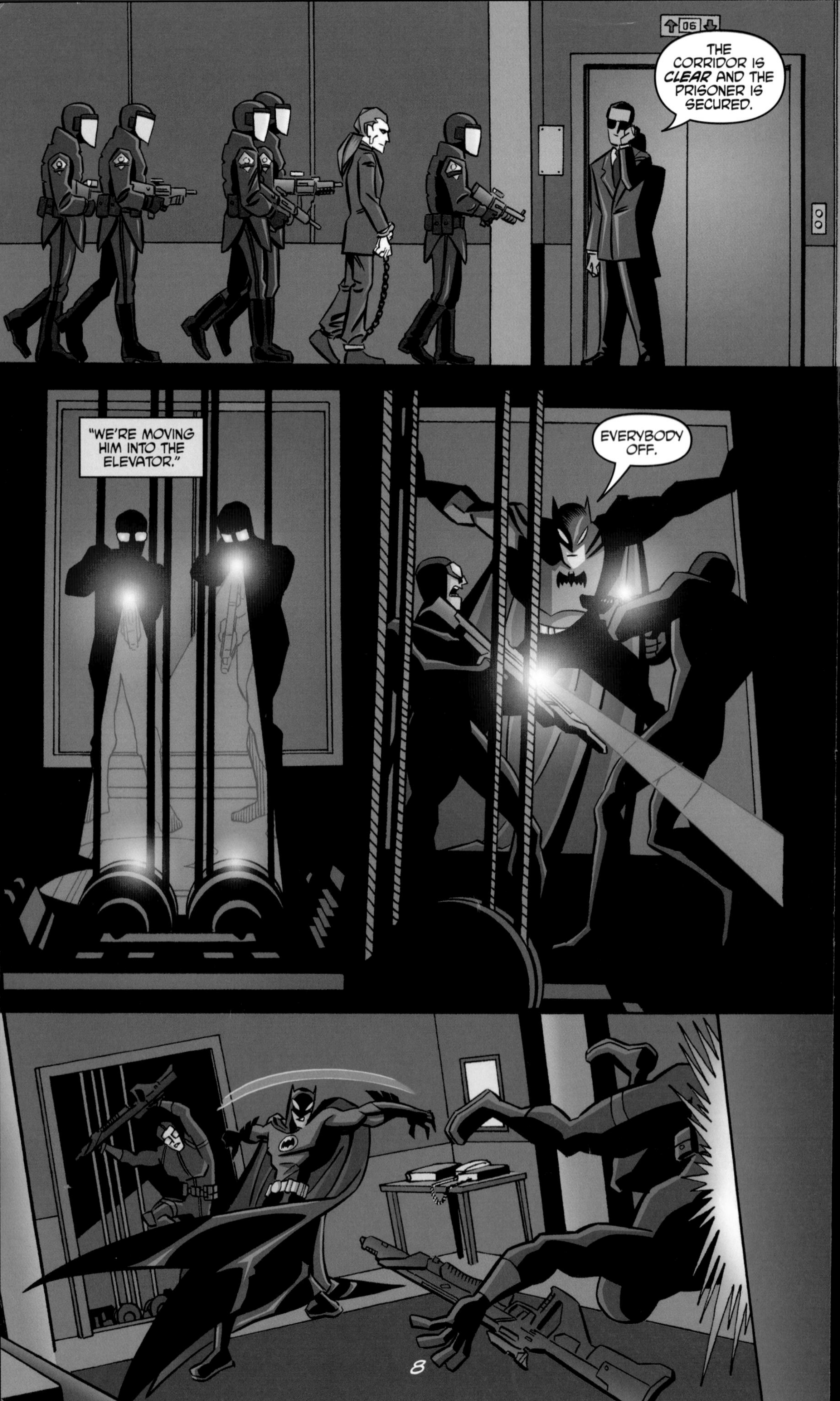

06
THE CORRIDOR IS CLEAR AND THE PRISONER IS SECURED.
"WE'RE MOVING HIM INTO THE ELEVATOR."
EVERYBODY OFF.

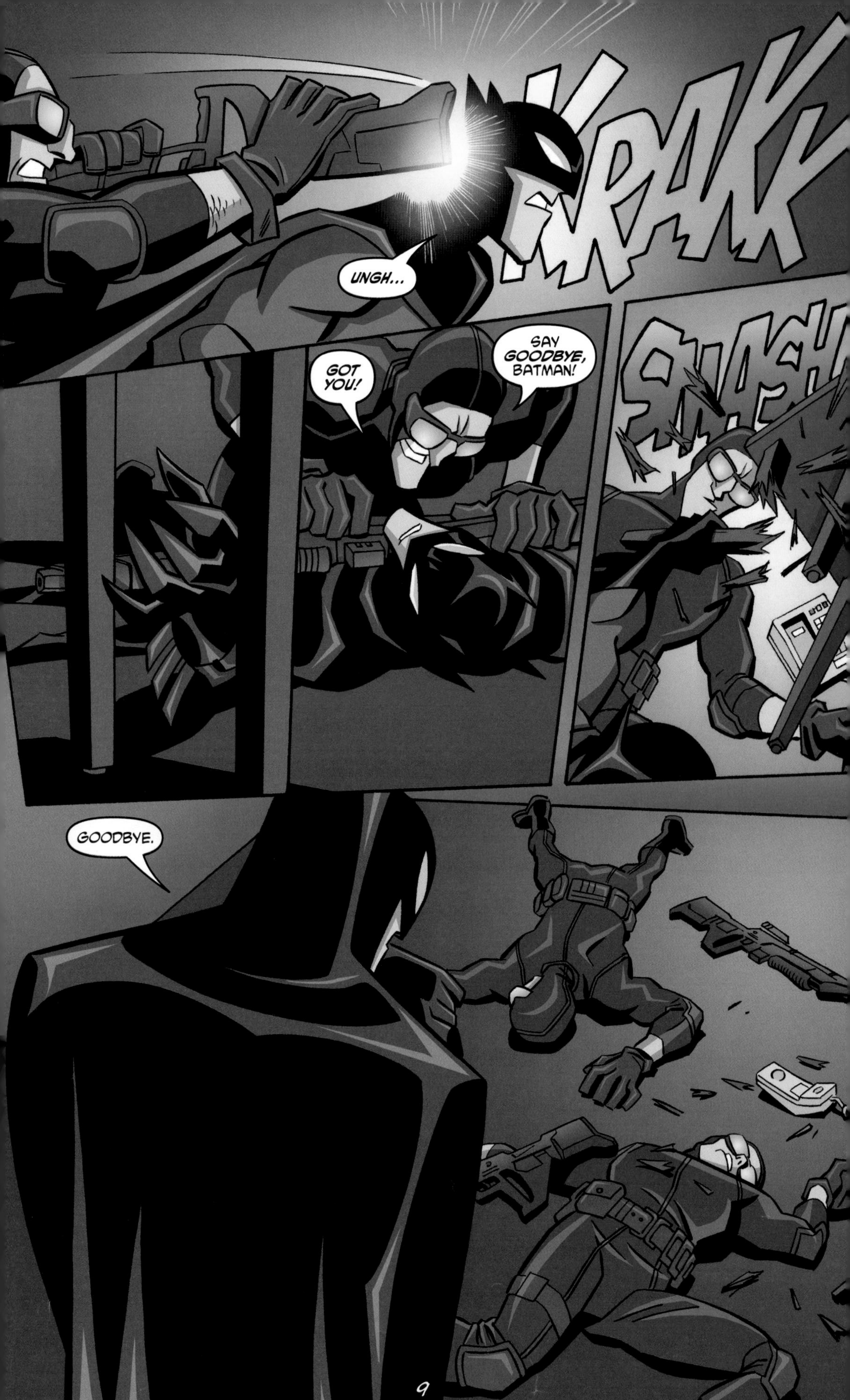
KRAK
UNGH...
GOT YOU!
SAY GOODBYE, BATMAN!
SMASH
GOODBYE.

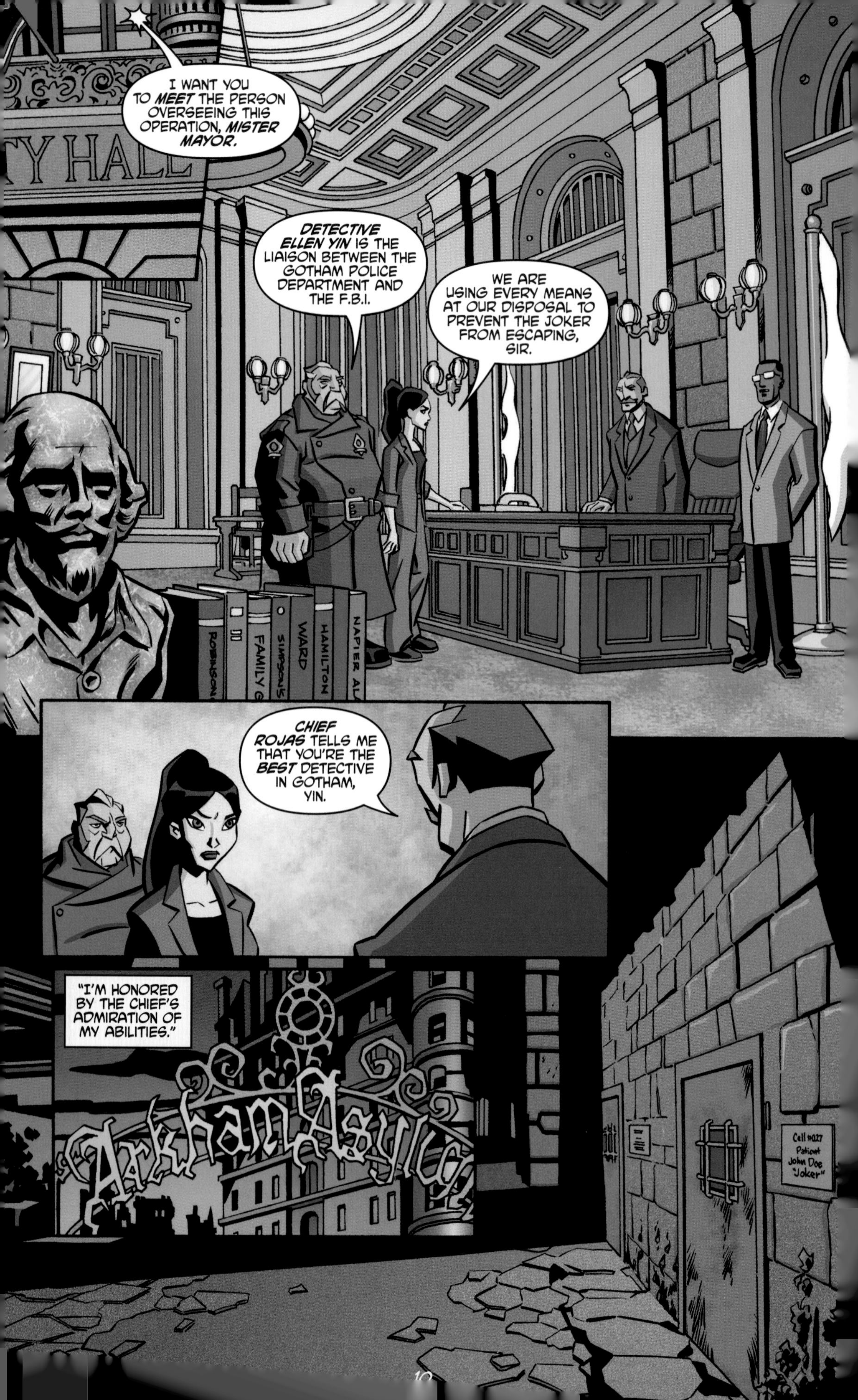

TY HALL
I WANT YOU TO MEET THE PERSON OVERSEEING THIS OPERATION, MISTER MAYOR.
DETECTIVE ELLEN YIN IS THE LIAISON BETWEEN THE GOTHAM POLICE DEPARTMENT AND THE F.B.I.
WE ARE USING EVERY MEANS AT OUR DISPOSAL TO PREVENT THE JOKER FROM ESCAPING, SIR.
ROBINSON
FAMILY
SIMPSONS
WARD
HAMILTON
NAPIER
CHIEF ROJAS TELLS ME THAT YOU'RE THE BEST DETECTIVE IN GOTHAM, YIN.
"I'M HONORED BY THE CHIEF'S ADMIRATION OF MY ABILITIES."
Cell #0227
Patient
John Doe
"Joker"

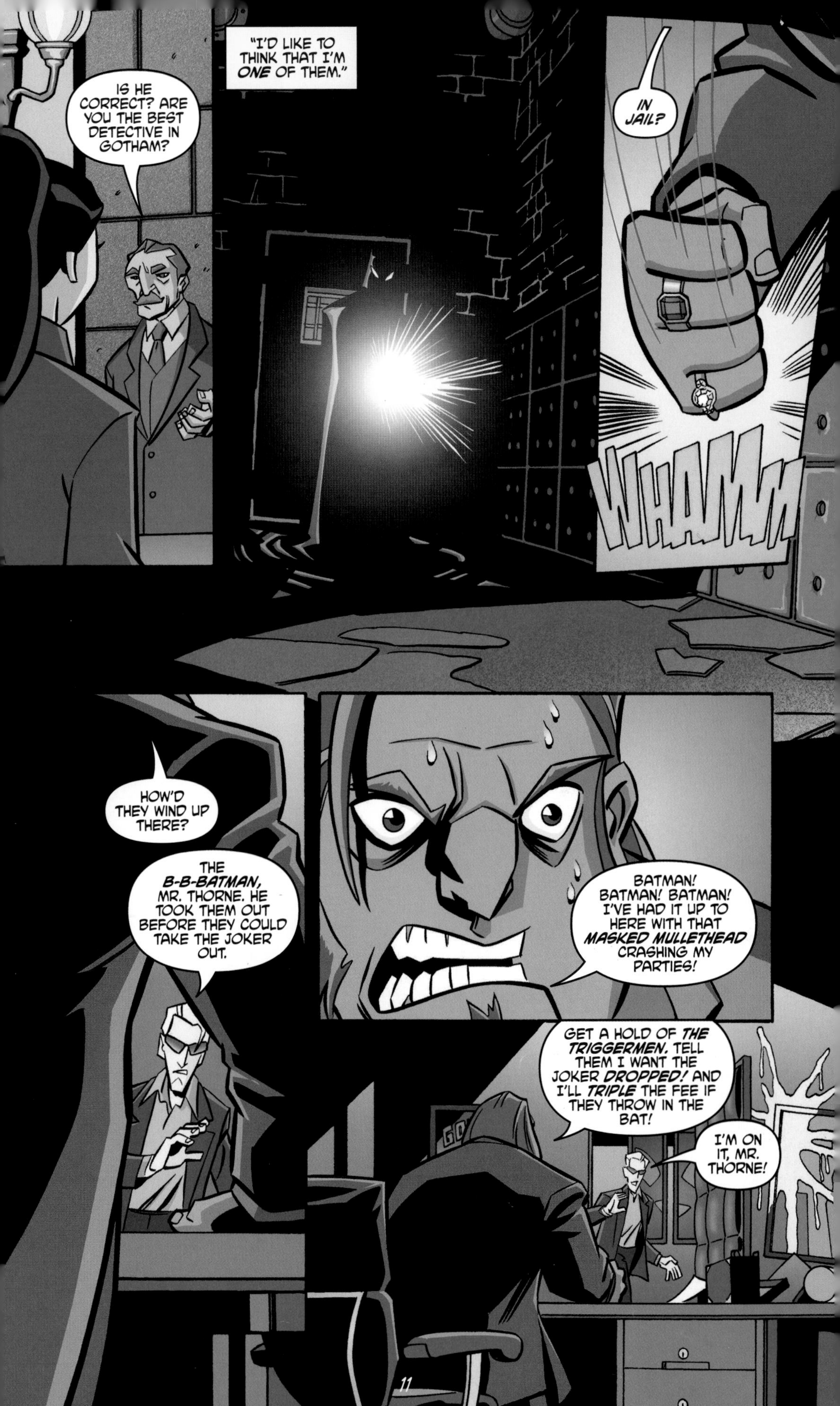

IS HE CORRECT? ARE YOU THE BEST DETECTIVE IN GOTHAM?
"I'D LIKE TO THINK THAT I'M ONE OF THEM."
IN JAIL?
WHAMM
HOW'D THEY WIND UP THERE?
THE B-B-BATMAN, MR. THORNE. HE TOOK THEM OUT BEFORE THEY COULD TAKE THE JOKER OUT.
BATMAN! BATMAN! BATMAN! I'VE HAD IT UP TO HERE WITH THAT MASKED MULLETHEAD CRASHING MY PARTIES!
GET A HOLD OF THE TRIGGERMEN. TELL THEM I WANT THE JOKER DROPPED! AND I'LL TRIPLE THE FEE IF THEY THROW IN THE BAT!
I'M ON IT, MR. THORNE!

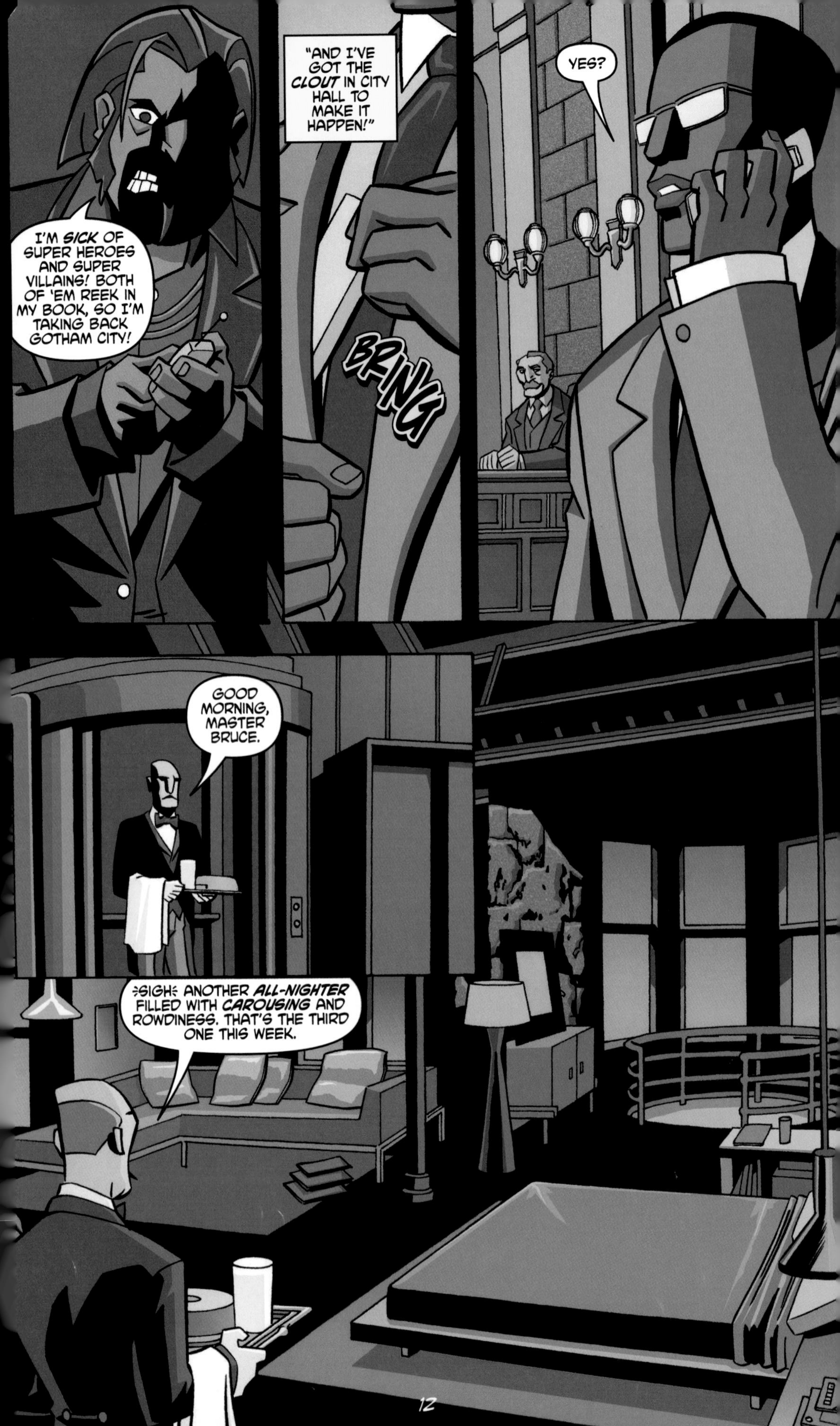
I'M SICK OF SUPER HEROES AND SUPER VILLAINS! BOTH OF 'EM REEK IN MY BOOK, SO I'M TAKING BACK GOTHAM CITY!
"AND I'VE GOT THE CLOUT IN CITY HALL TO MAKE IT HAPPEN!"
BRING
YES?
GOOD MORNING, MASTER BRUCE.
SIGH ANOTHER ALL-NIGHTER FILLED WITH CAROUSING AND ROWDINESS. THAT'S THE THIRD ONE THIS WEEK.

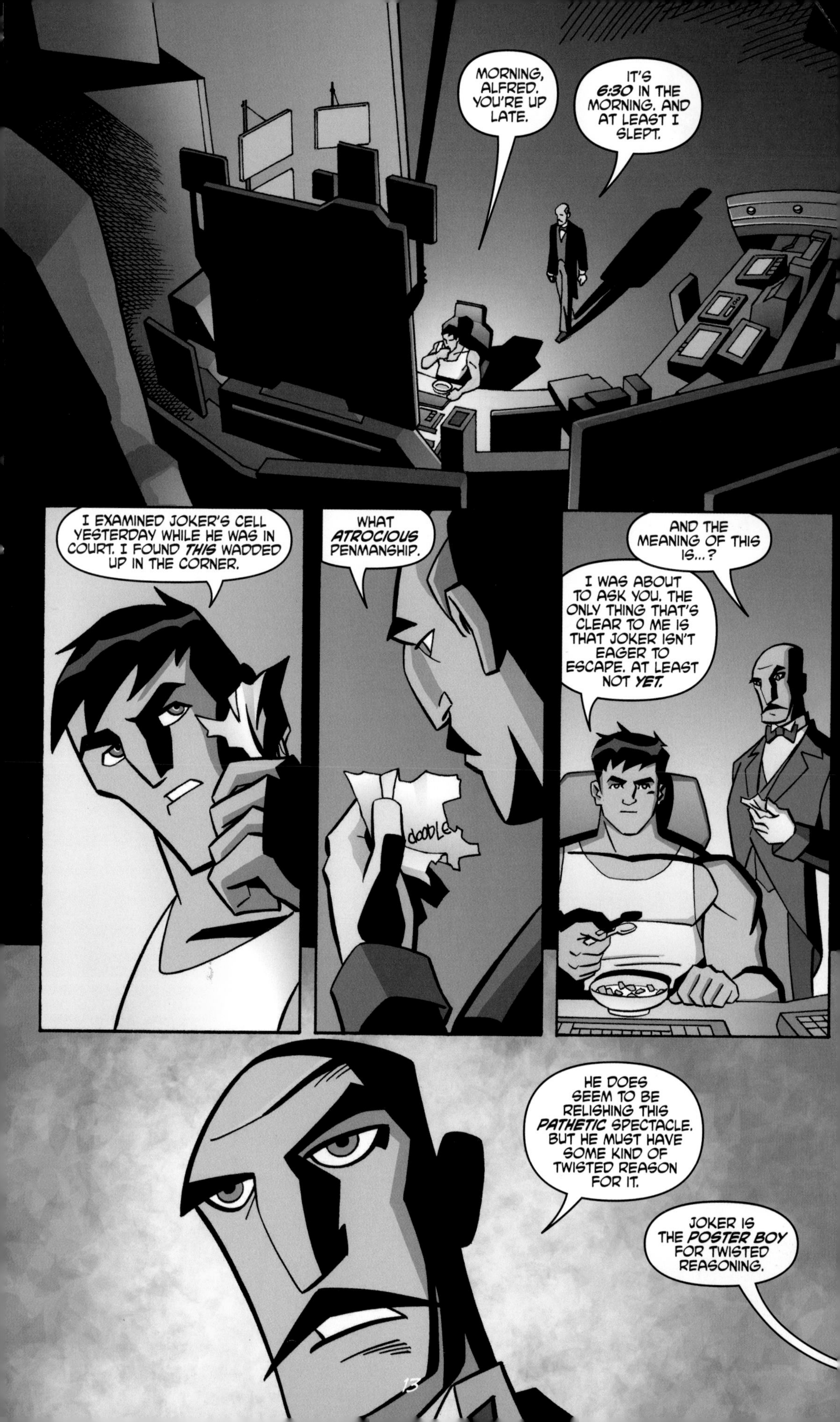
MORNING, ALFRED. YOU'RE UP LATE.
IT'S 6:30 IN THE MORNING. AND AT LEAST I SLEPT.
I EXAMINED JOKER'S CELL YESTERDAY WHILE HE WAS IN COURT. I FOUND THIS WADDED UP IN THE CORNER.
WHAT ATROCIOUS PENMANSHIP.
doodle
AND THE MEANING OF THIS IS...?
I WAS ABOUT TO ASK YOU. THE ONLY THING THAT'S CLEAR TO ME IS THAT JOKER ISN'T EAGER TO ESCAPE. AT LEAST NOT YET.
HE DOES SEEM TO BE RELISHING THIS PATHETIC SPECTACLE. BUT HE MUST HAVE SOME KIND OF TWISTED REASON FOR IT.
JOKER IS THE POSTER BOY FOR TWISTED REASONING.

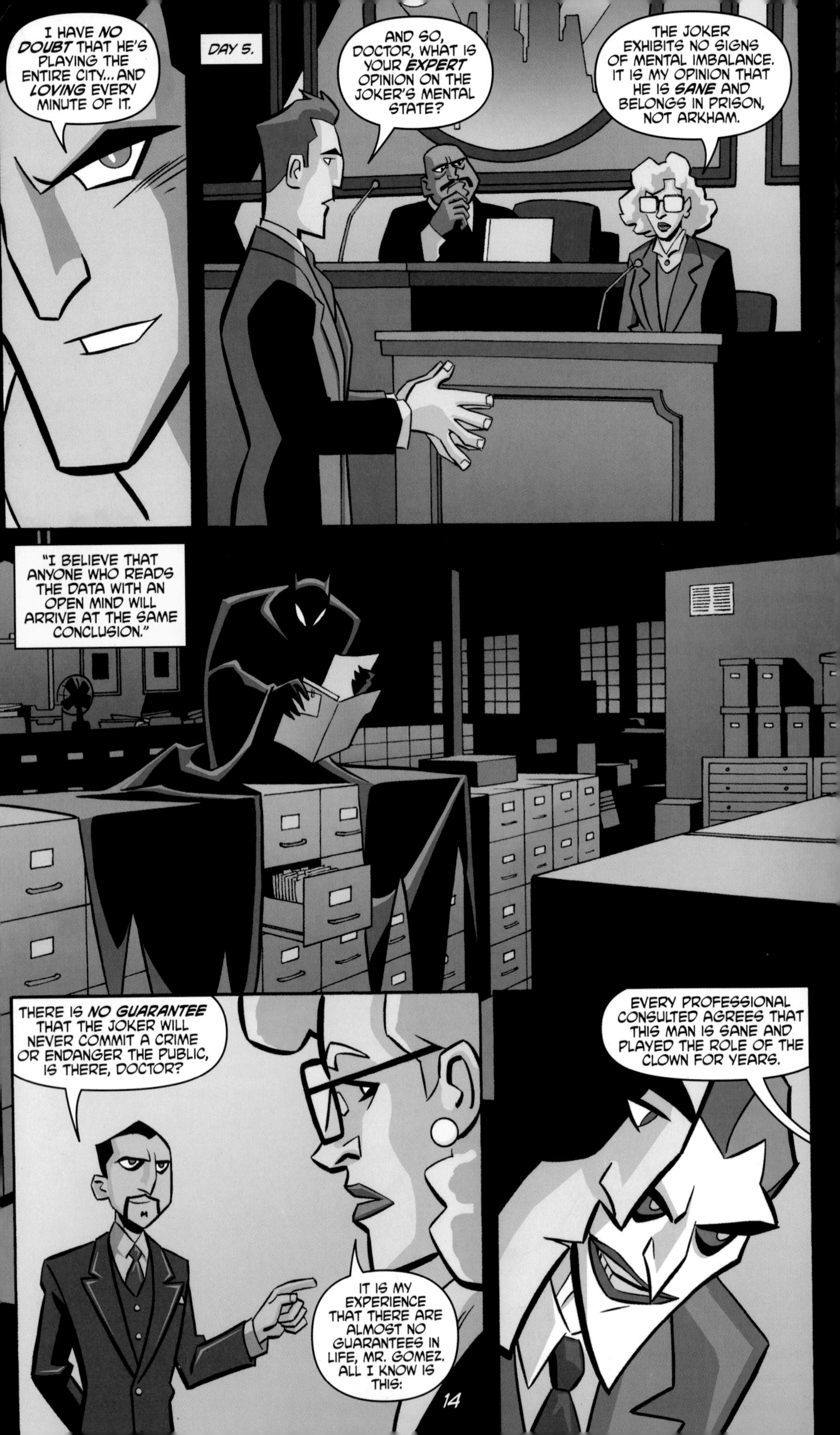
I HAVE NO DOUBT THAT HE'S PLAYING THE ENTIRE CITY... AND LOVING EVERY MINUTE OF IT.
DAY 5.
AND SO, DOCTOR, WHAT IS YOUR EXPERT OPINION ON THE JOKER'S MENTAL STATE?
THE JOKER EXHIBITS NO SIGNS OF MENTAL IMBALANCE. IT IS MY OPINION THAT HE IS SANE AND BELONGS IN PRISON, NOT ARKHAM.
"I BELIEVE THAT ANYONE WHO READS THE DATA WITH AN OPEN MIND WILL ARRIVE AT THE SAME CONCLUSION."
THERE IS NO GUARANTEE THAT THE JOKER WILL NEVER COMMIT A CRIME OR ENDANGER THE PUBLIC, IS THERE, DOCTOR?
IT IS MY EXPERIENCE THAT THERE ARE ALMOST NO GUARANTEES IN LIFE, MR. GOMEZ. ALL I KNOW IS THIS:
EVERY PROFESSIONAL CONSULTED AGREES THAT THIS MAN IS SANE AND PLAYED THE ROLE OF THE CLOWN FOR YEARS.

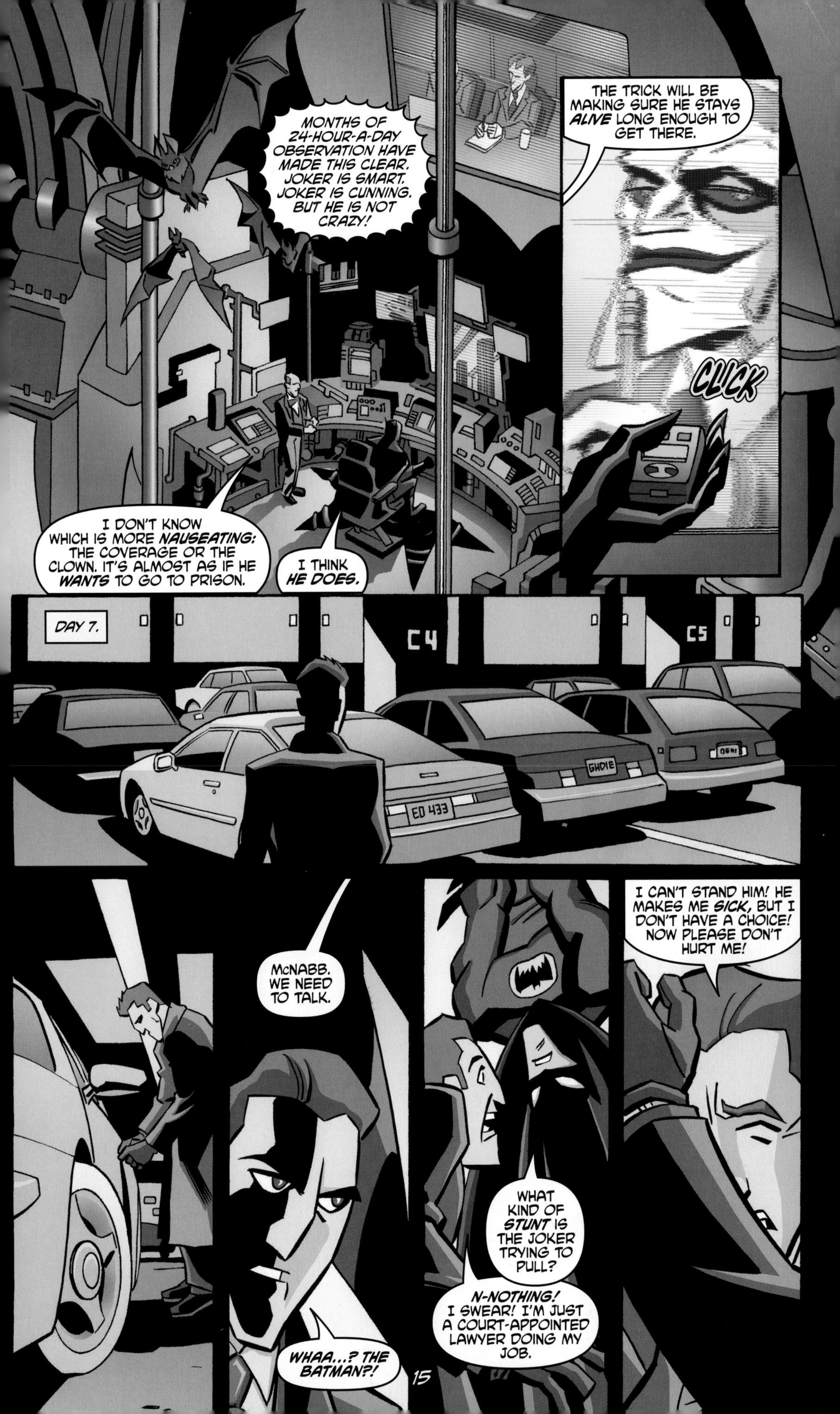

MONTHS OF 24-HOUR-A-DAY OBSERVATION HAVE MADE THIS CLEAR. JOKER IS SMART. JOKER IS CUNNING. BUT HE IS NOT CRAZY!
THE TRICK WILL BE MAKING SURE HE STAYS ALIVE LONG ENOUGH TO GET THERE.
CLICK
I DON'T KNOW WHICH IS MORE NAUSEATING: THE COVERAGE OR THE CLOWN. IT'S ALMOST AS IF HE WANTS TO GO TO PRISON.
I THINK HE DOES.
DAY 7.
C4
C5
ED 433
McNABB. WE NEED TO TALK.
WHAA...? THE BATMAN?!
WHAT KIND OF STUNT IS THE JOKER TRYING TO PULL?
N-NOTHING! I SWEAR! I'M JUST A COURT-APPOINTED LAWYER DOING MY JOB.
I CAN'T STAND HIM! HE MAKES ME SICK, BUT I DON'T HAVE A CHOICE! NOW PLEASE DON'T HURT ME!

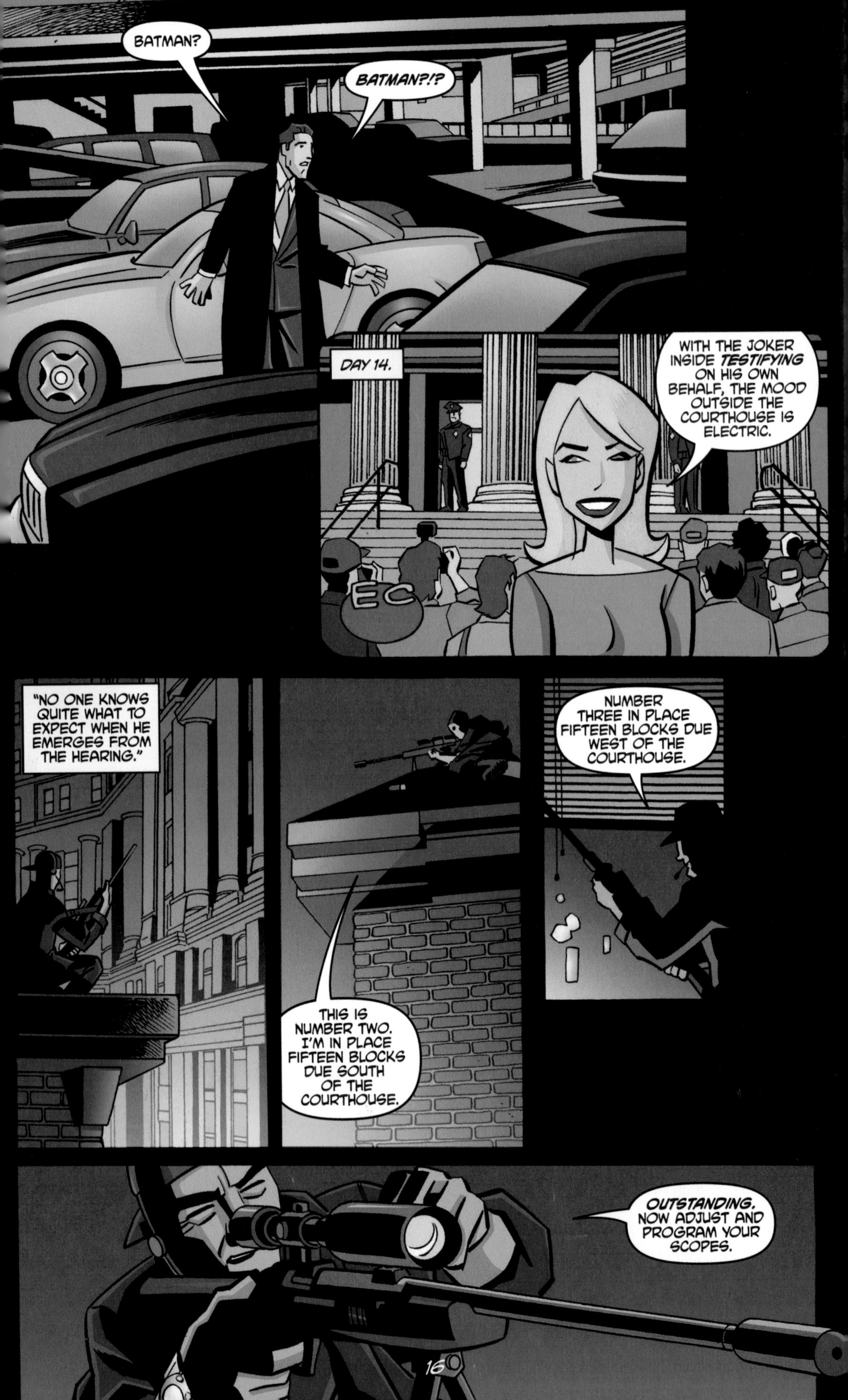
BATMAN?
BATMAN?!?
DAY 14.
WITH THE JOKER INSIDE TESTIFYING ON HIS OWN BEHALF, THE MOOD OUTSIDE THE COURTHOUSE IS ELECTRIC.
EC
"NO ONE KNOWS QUITE WHAT TO EXPECT WHEN HE EMERGES FROM THE HEARING."
THIS IS NUMBER TWO. I'M IN PLACE FIFTEEN BLOCKS DUE SOUTH OF THE COURTHOUSE.
NUMBER THREE IN PLACE FIFTEEN BLOCKS DUE WEST OF THE COURTHOUSE.
OUTSTANDING. NOW ADJUST AND PROGRAM YOUR SCOPES.

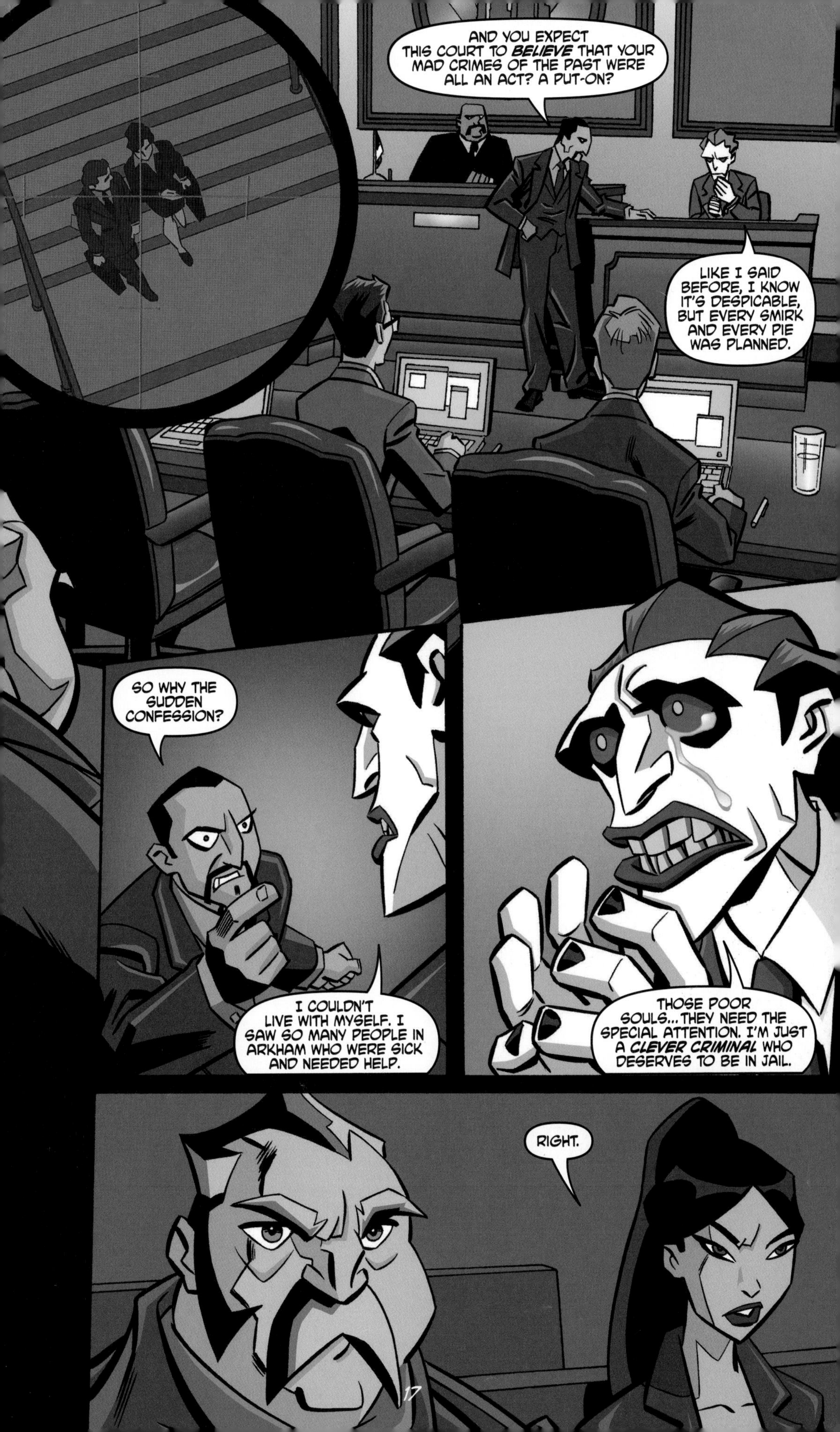
AND YOU EXPECT THIS COURT TO *BELIEVE* THAT YOUR MAD CRIMES OF THE PAST WERE ALL AN ACT? A PUT-ON?
LIKE I SAID BEFORE, I KNOW IT'S DESPICABLE, BUT EVERY SMIRK AND EVERY PIE WAS PLANNED.
SO WHY THE SUDDEN CONFESSION?
I COULDN'T LIVE WITH MYSELF. I SAW SO MANY PEOPLE IN ARKHAM WHO WERE SICK AND NEEDED HELP.
THOSE POOR SOULS... THEY NEED THE SPECIAL ATTENTION. I'M JUST A *CLEVER CRIMINAL* WHO DESERVES TO BE IN JAIL.
RIGHT.

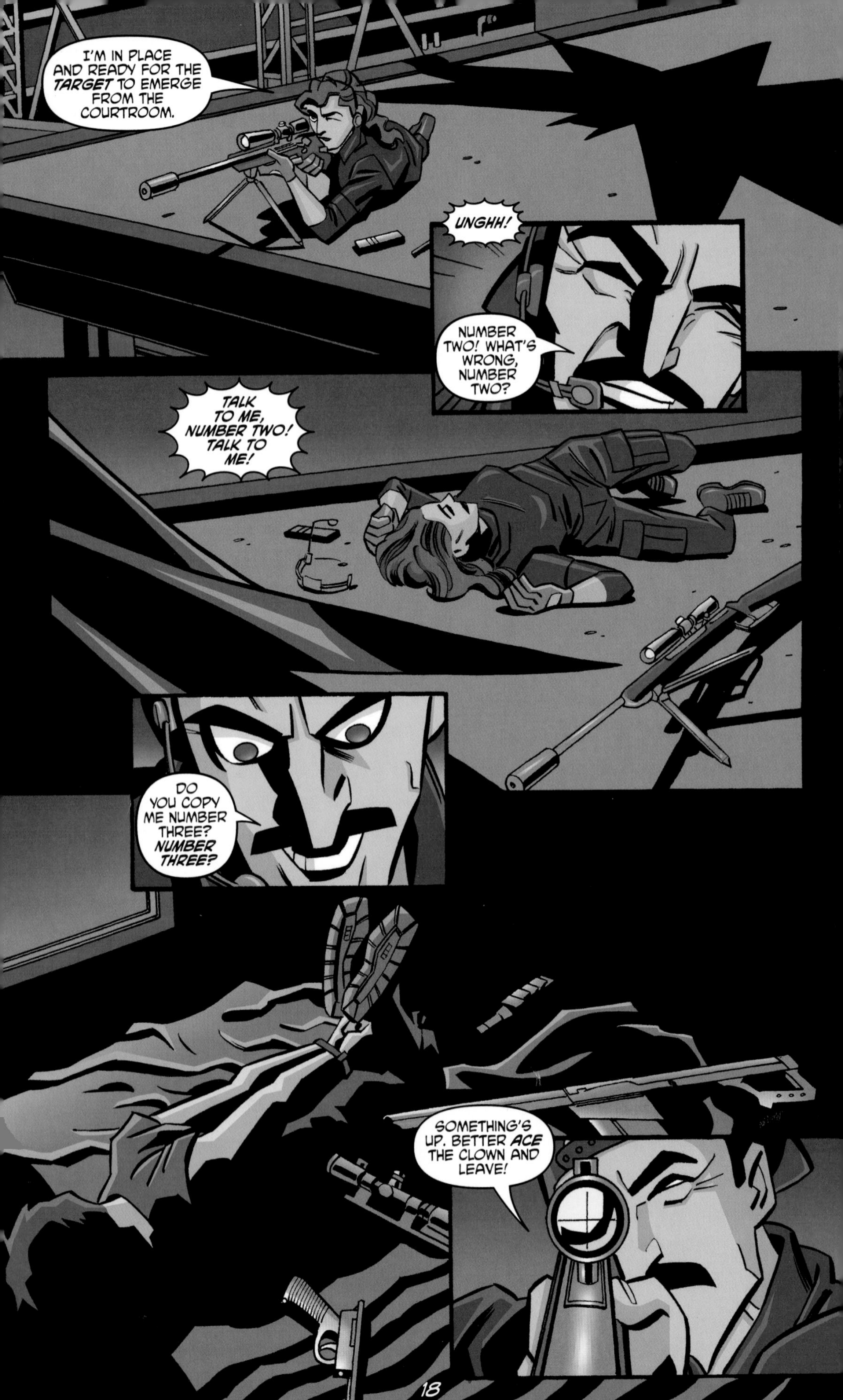
I'M IN PLACE AND READY FOR THE TARGET TO EMERGE FROM THE COURTROOM.
UNGHH!
NUMBER TWO! WHAT'S WRONG, NUMBER TWO?
TALK TO ME, NUMBER TWO! TALK TO ME!
DO YOU COPY ME NUMBER THREE? NUMBER THREE?
SOMETHING'S UP. BETTER ACE THE CLOWN AND LEAVE!

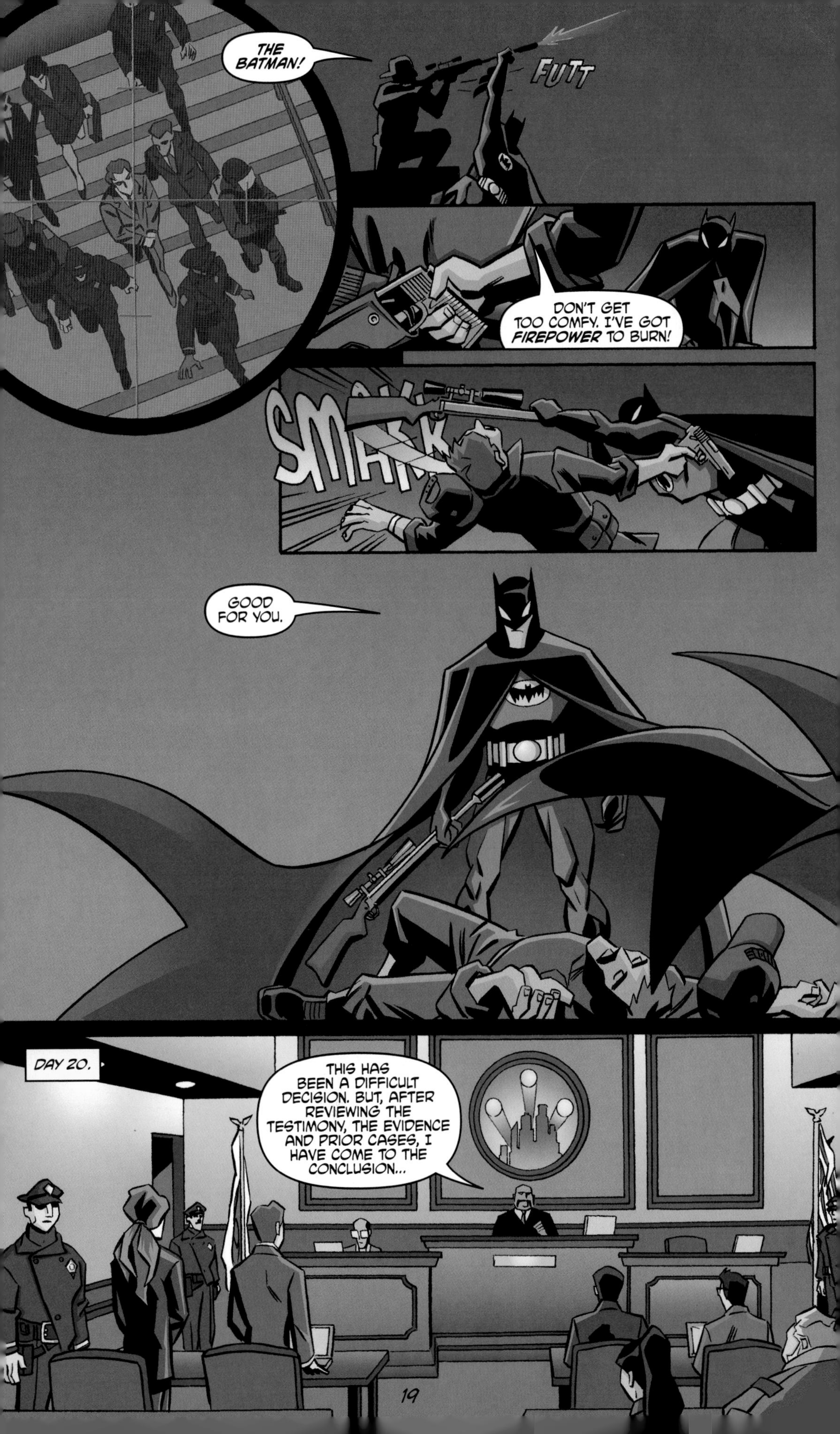
THE BATMAN!
FUTT
DON'T GET TOO COMFY. I'VE GOT *FIREPOWER* TO BURN!
SMAK
GOOD FOR YOU.
DAY 20.
THIS HAS BEEN A DIFFICULT DECISION. BUT, AFTER REVIEWING THE TESTIMONY, THE EVIDENCE AND PRIOR CASES, I HAVE COME TO THE CONCLUSION...

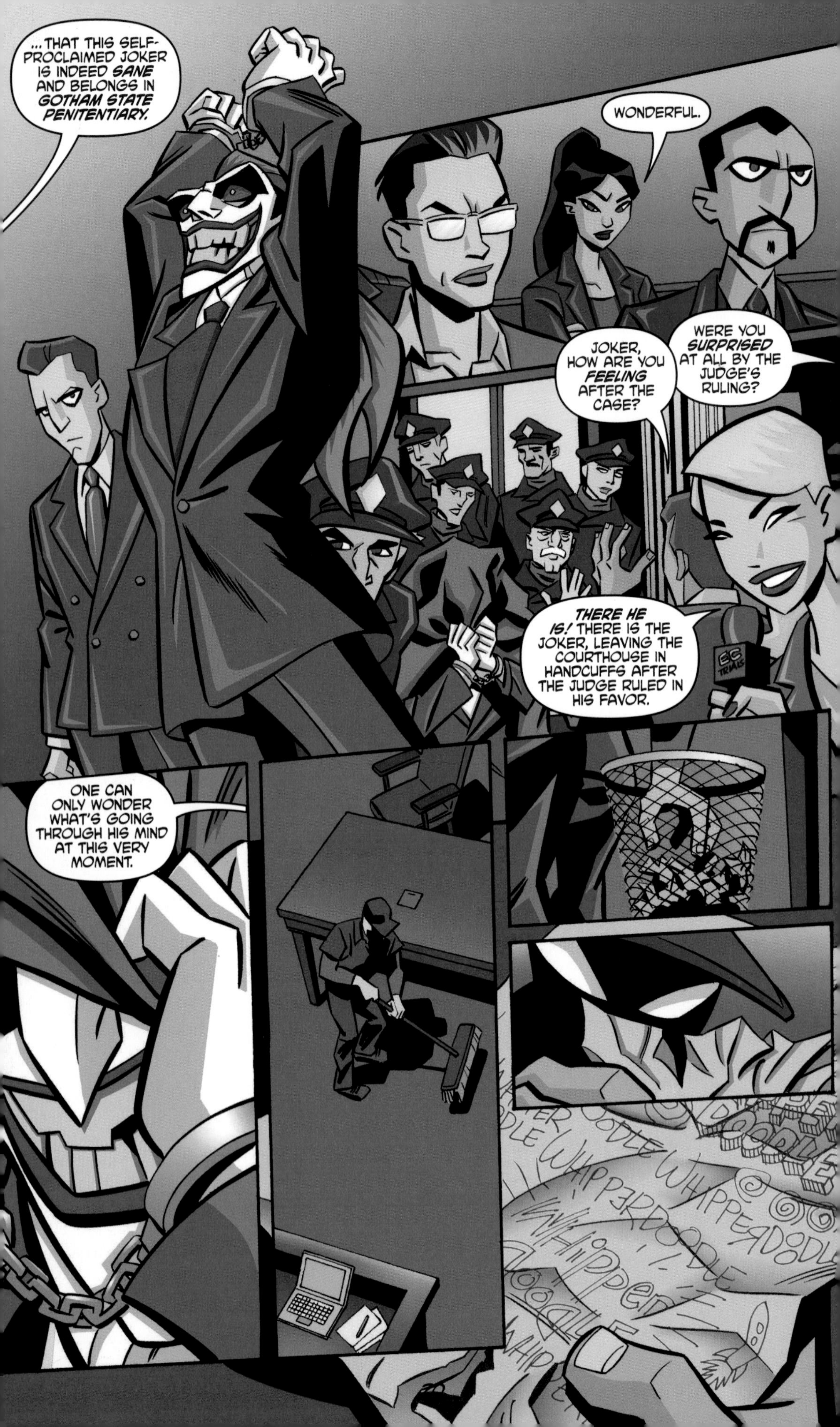
...THAT THIS SELF-PROCLAIMED JOKER IS INDEED SANE AND BELONGS IN GOTHAM STATE PENITENTIARY.
WONDERFUL.
JOKER, HOW ARE YOU FEELING AFTER THE CASE?
WERE YOU SURPRISED AT ALL BY THE JUDGE'S RULING?
THERE HE IS! THERE IS THE JOKER, LEAVING THE COURTHOUSE IN HANDCUFFS AFTER THE JUDGE RULED IN HIS FAVOR.
ONE CAN ONLY WONDER WHAT'S GOING THROUGH HIS MIND AT THIS VERY MOMENT.

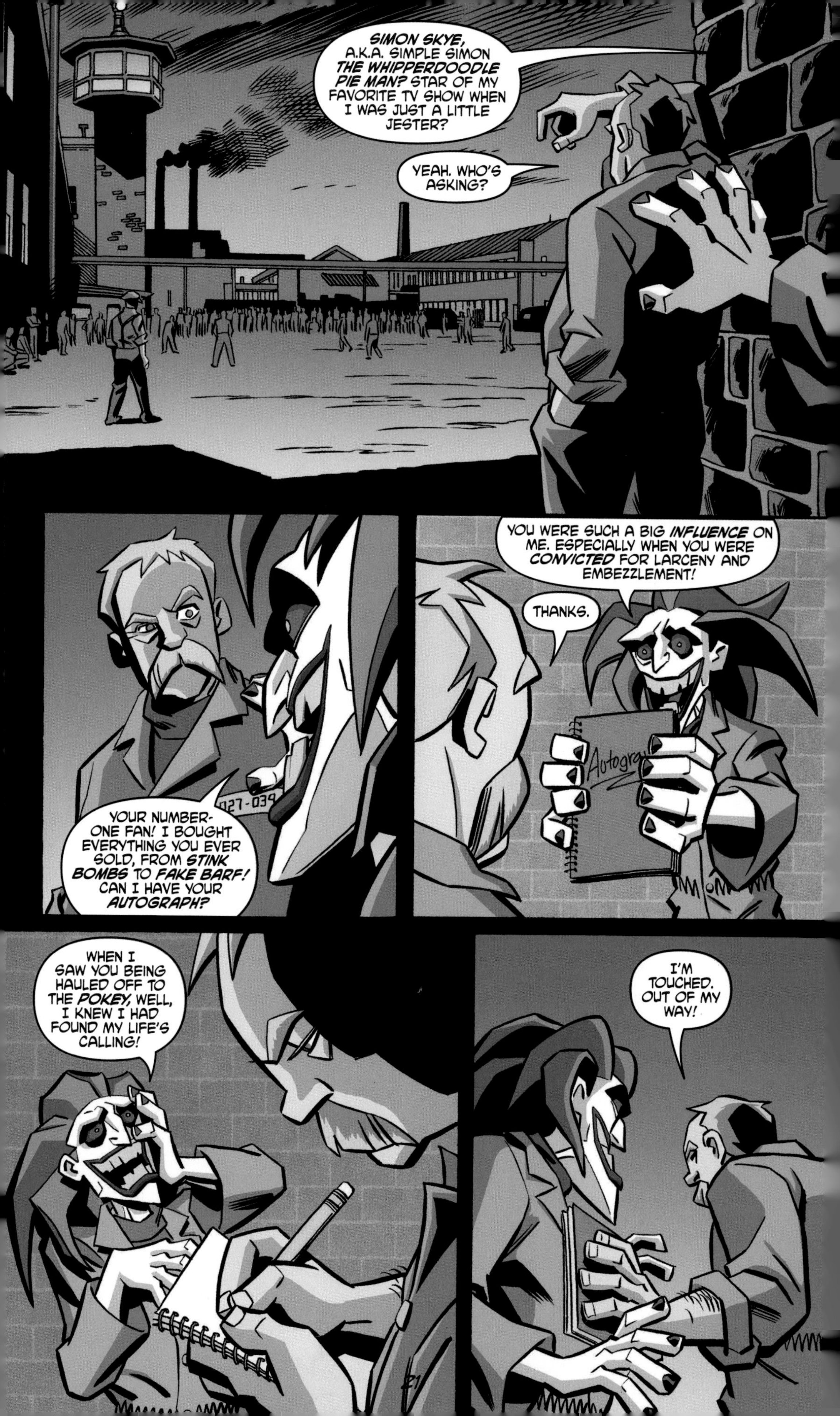
SIMON SKYE, A.K.A. SIMPLE SIMON THE WHIPPERDOODLE PIE MAN? STAR OF MY FAVORITE TV SHOW WHEN I WAS JUST A LITTLE JESTER?
YEAH. WHO'S ASKING?
YOUR NUMBER-ONE FAN! I BOUGHT EVERYTHING YOU EVER SOLD, FROM STINK BOMBS TO FAKE BARF! CAN I HAVE YOUR AUTOGRAPH?
YOU WERE SUCH A BIG INFLUENCE ON ME. ESPECIALLY WHEN YOU WERE CONVICTED FOR LARCENY AND EMBEZZLEMENT!
THANKS.
WHEN I SAW YOU BEING HAULED OFF TO THE POKEY, WELL, I KNEW I HAD FOUND MY LIFE'S CALLING!
I'M TOUCHED. OUT OF MY WAY!

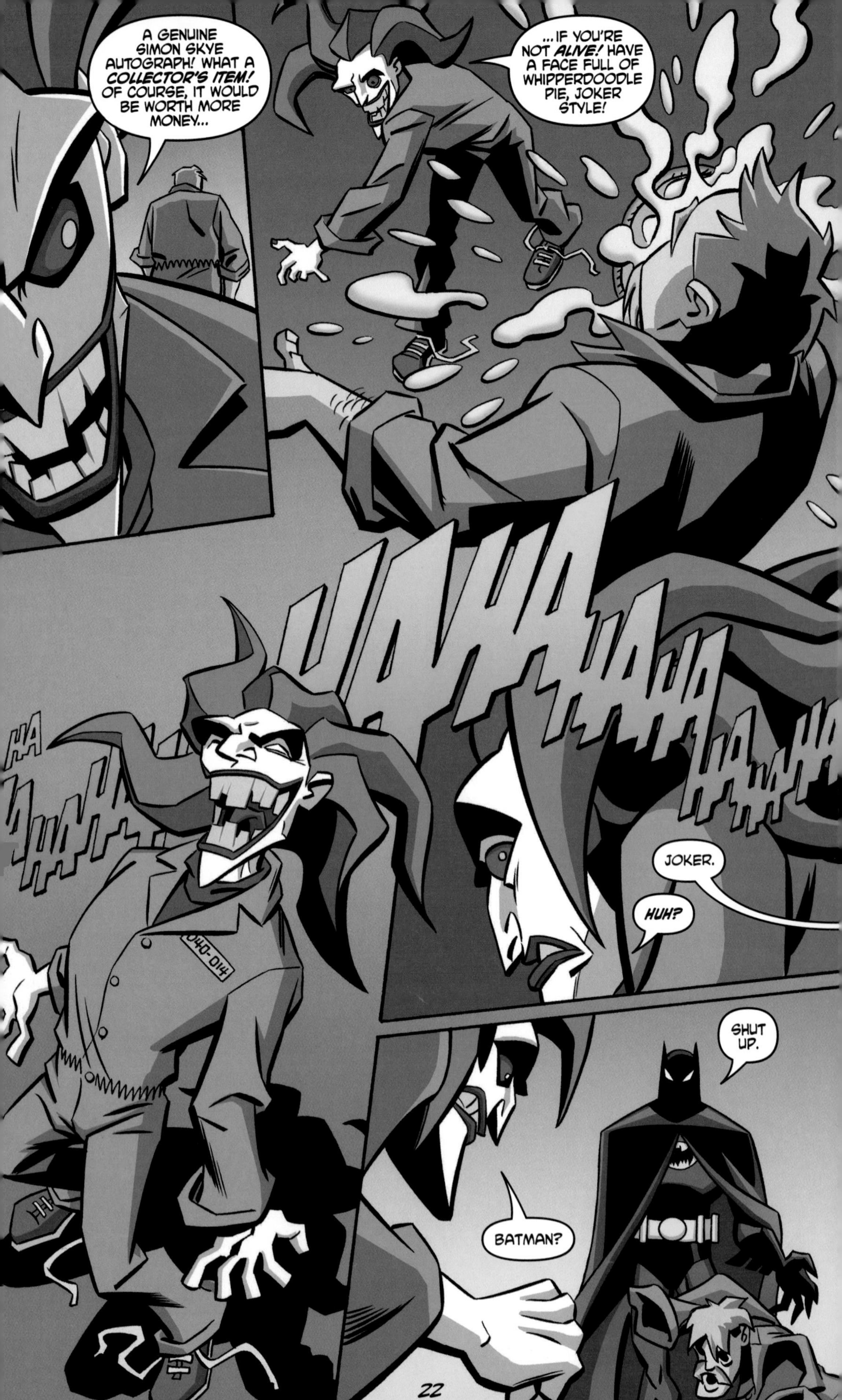
A GENUINE SIMON SKYE AUTOGRAPH! WHAT A COLLECTOR'S ITEM! OF COURSE, IT WOULD BE WORTH MORE MONEY...
...IF YOU'RE NOT ALIVE! HAVE A FACE FULL OF WHIPPERDOODLE PIE, JOKER STYLE!
HAHAHA
HAHAHA
HA
HAHAHA
040-014
JOKER.
HUH?
SHUT UP.
BATMAN?

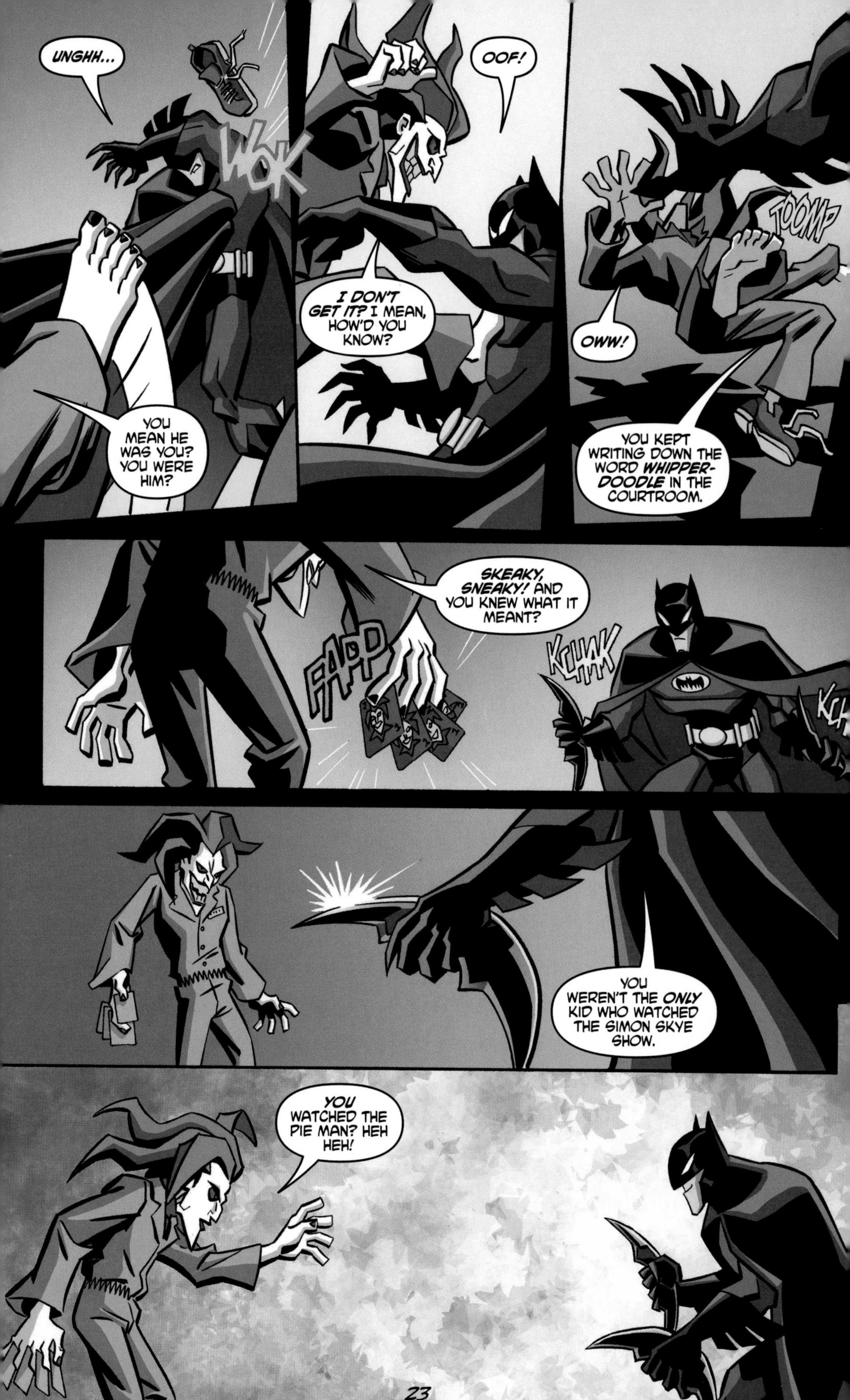
UNGHH...
WOK
OOF!
I DON'T GET IT? I MEAN, HOW'D YOU KNOW?
YOU MEAN HE WAS YOU? YOU WERE HIM?
TOOMP
OWW!
YOU KEPT WRITING DOWN THE WORD WHIPPER-DOODLE IN THE COURTROOM.
SKEAKY, SNEAKY! AND YOU KNEW WHAT IT MEANT?
FAPP
KCHAK
YOU WEREN'T THE ONLY KID WHO WATCHED THE SIMON SKYE SHOW.
YOU WATCHED THE PIE MAN? HEH HEH!

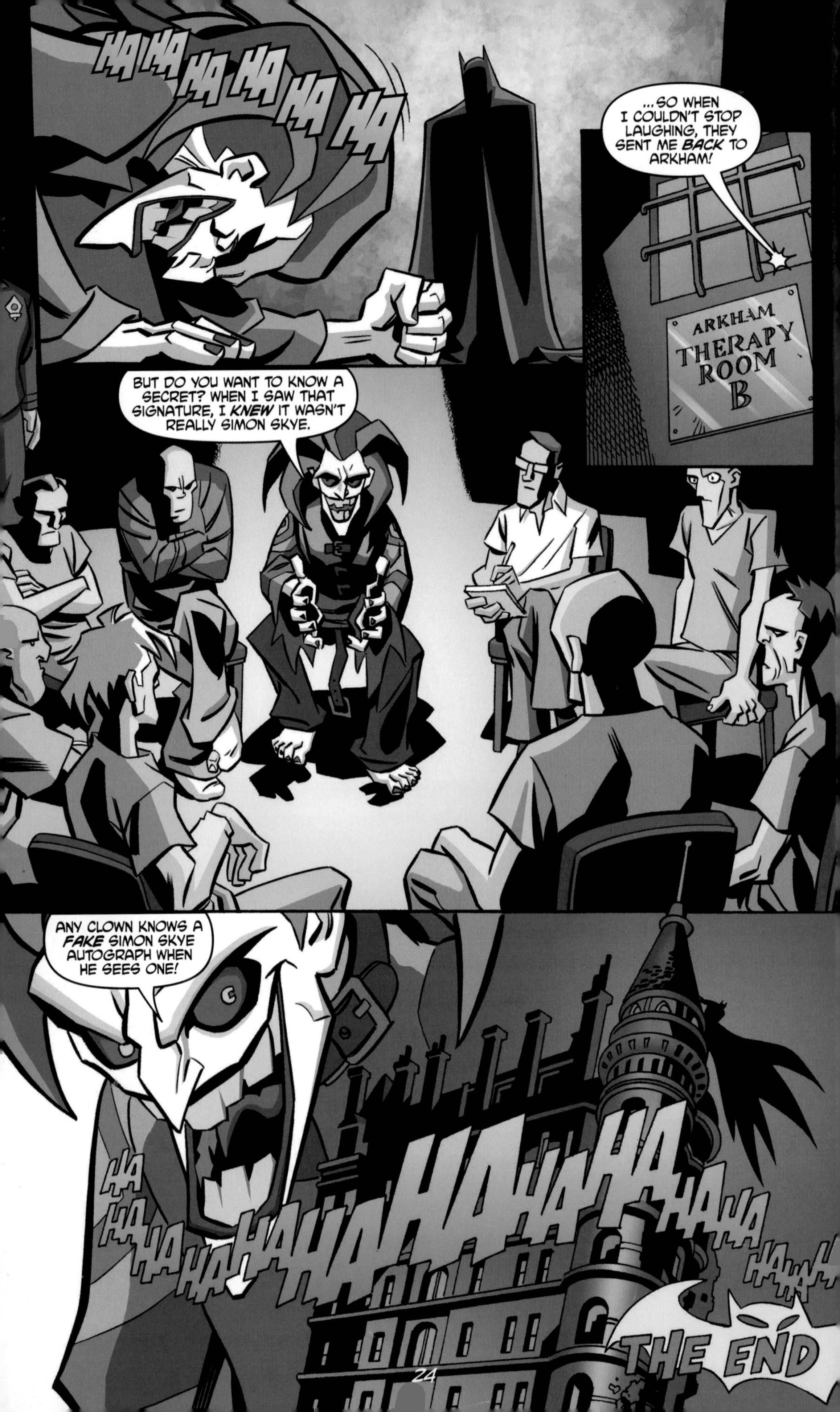
HA HA HA HA HA HA HA HA
...SO WHEN I COULDN'T STOP LAUGHING, THEY SENT ME BACK TO ARKHAM!
ARKHAM THERAPY ROOM B
BUT DO YOU WANT TO KNOW A SECRET? WHEN I SAW THAT SIGNATURE, I KNEW IT WASN'T REALLY SIMON SKYE.
ANY CLOWN KNOWS A FAKE SIMON SKYE AUTOGRAPH WHEN HE SEES ONE!
HA HA HA HA HA HA HA HA HA HA HA HA HA HA HA
THE END

CREATORS

BILL MATHENY WRITER

Along with comics like THE BATMAN STRIKES, Bill Matheny has
written for TV series including KRYPTO THE SUPERDOG, WHERE'S
WALDO, A PUP NAMED SCOOBY-DOO, and many others.

CHRISTOPHER JONES PENCILLER

Christopher Jones is an artist who has worked for DC Comics,
Image, Malibu, Caliber, and Sundragon Comics.

TERRY BEATTY INKER

Terry Beatty has inked THE BATMAN STRIKES! and BATMAN:
THE BRAVE AND THE BOLD as well as several other DC Comics
graphic novels.

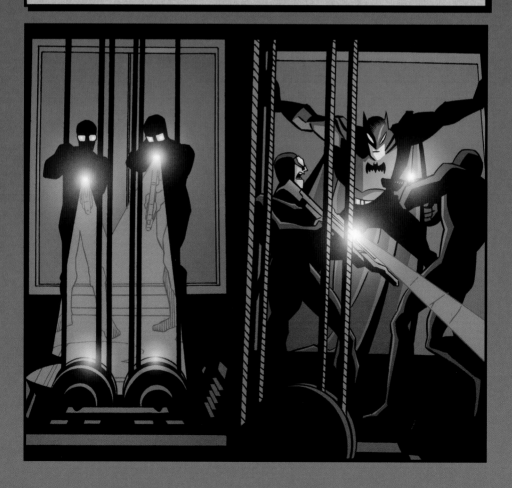

GLOSSARY

embezzlement (em-BEZ-uhl-ment)--the act of secretly stealing money from a workplace or organization

larceny (LAHR-suh-nee)--theft

liaison (lee-AY-zahn)--a person who helps two groups work together

penitentiary (pen-i-TEN-chur-ee)--a prison for people found guilty of serious crimes

plaintiff (PLAYN-tiff)--a person who brings a case against another in court

restrictive (ri-STRIKT-iv)--keeping within bounds

sanity (SAN-i-tee)--mental health

stabilized (STAY-buhl-ized)--became steady or firm

surveillance (sur-VAYL-uhnss)--close watch

testimony (TES-tuh-moh-nee)--a statement given by a witness or expert in court

VISUAL QUESTIONS & PROMPTS

1. Why do you think the artists chose to display the title in such an unusual font? Does it make you approach the book differently?

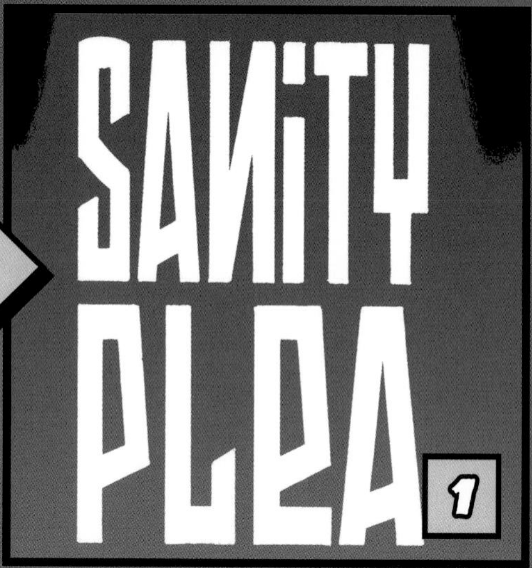
SANITY PLEA
1

2. What is happening in this panel? Are you able to predict what will happen next?

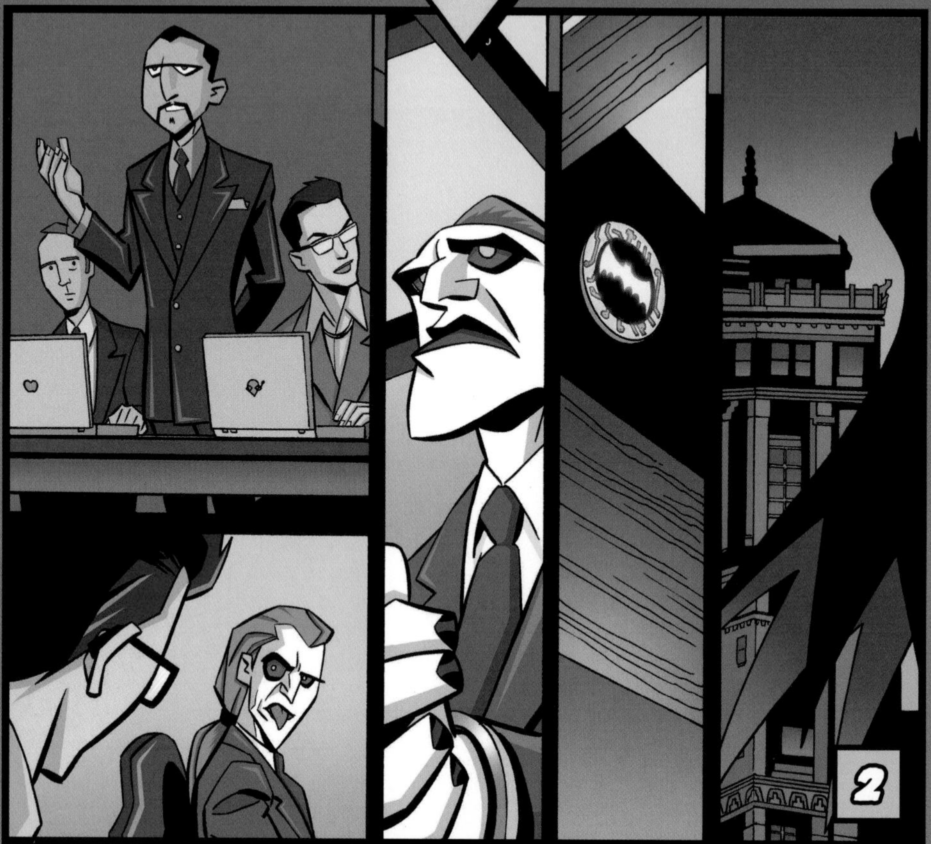
2

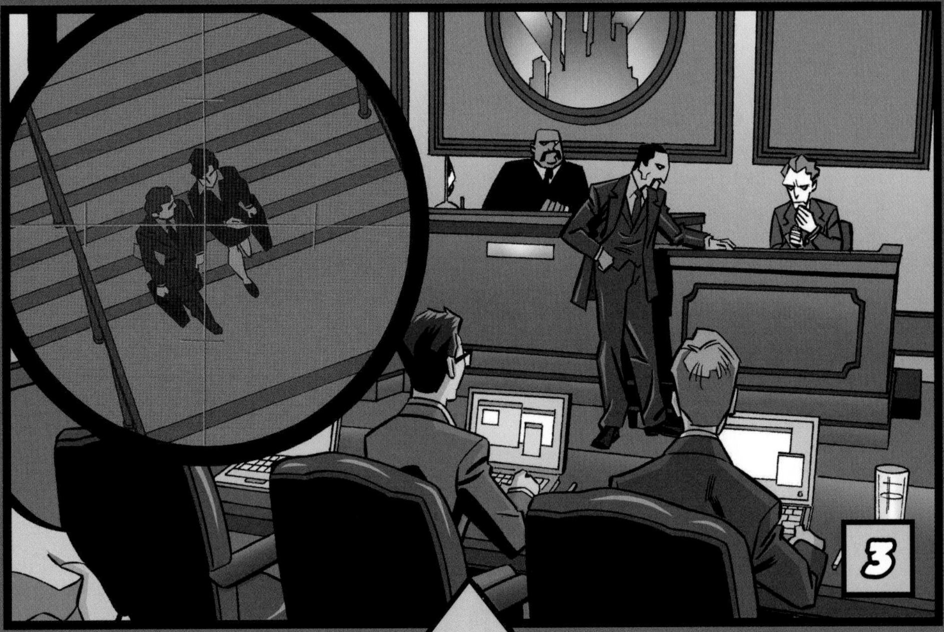
3

3. Why do you think the artists included the circular panel with crosshairs within the larger panel of the court? How does it influence how you view the courthouse scene?

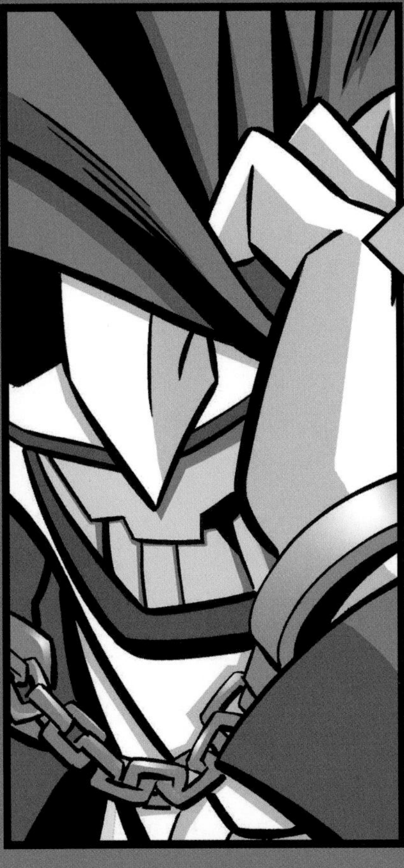

4. Why do you think this panel is zoomed in on Joker's face? What does it add to the scene?

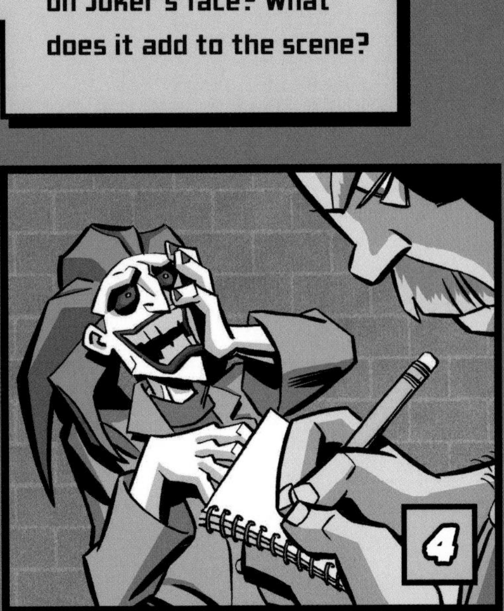
4

READ THEM ALL

THE BATMAN® STRIKES!

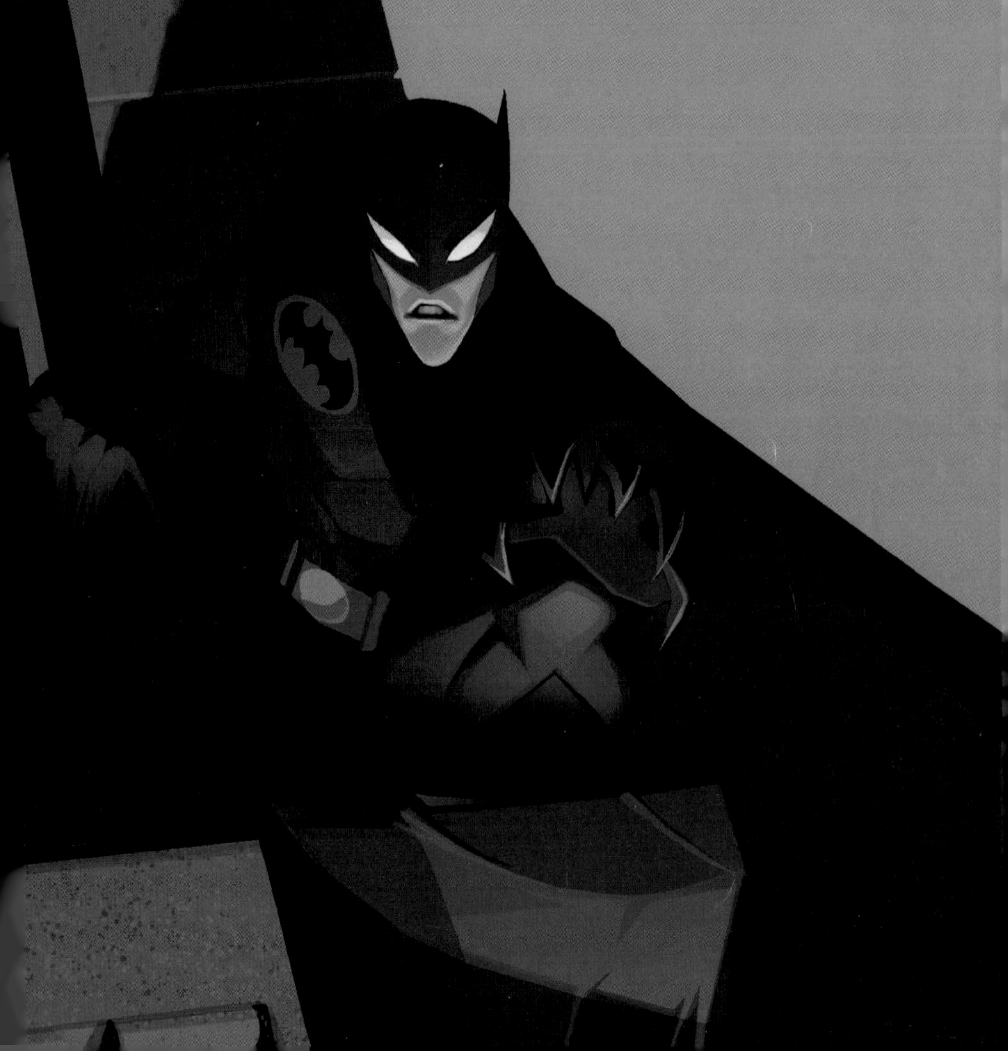

W9-BFO-402

3/29 One

DAILY LIFE

A Medieval Castle

Marcia S. Gresko

KIDHAVEN
PRESS™

THOMSON
————✦————™
GALE

San Diego • Detroit • New York • San Francisco • Cleveland
New Haven, Conn. • Waterville, Maine • London • Munich

THOMSON

GALE

Picture Credits

Cover photo: © Réunion des Musées Nationaux/Art Resource
© Alinari/Art Resource, 8, 27
The Art Archive/British Library, 30
The Art Archive/College St. Michel Fribourg Switzerland/Dagli Orti, 41
The Art Archive/Musée du Chateau de Versailles/Dagli Orti, 34
The Art Archive/Real biblioteca de lo Escorial/Dagli Orti, 31, 40
British Library, London/Bridgeman Art Library, 25
Christie's Images/Bridgeman Art Library, 21
© Corel Corporation, 5, 38
Giraudon/Bridgeman Art Library, 11, 17
© Hulton/Archive by Getty Images, 6
Mary Evans Picture Library, 19, 23
Brandy Noon, 36, 37
Private Collection/Bridgeman Art Library, 13
© Scala/Art Resource, 15
The Stapleton Collection/Bridgeman Art Library, 29
Victoria and Albert Museum, London/Bridgeman Art Library, 9

For more information, contact
KidHaven Press
27500 Drake Rd.
Farmington Hills, MI 48331-3535
Or you can visit our Internet site at http://www.gale.com

LIBRARY OF CONGRESS CATALOGING-IN-PUBLICATION DATA

Gresko, Marcia S.
A medieval castle / by Marcia S. Gresko.
p. cm.—(Daily life series)
Includes bibliographical references and index.
Summary: Describes the layout, construction, and daily life of the inhabitants of a medieval castle.
ISBN 0-7377-1363-1 (hardback : alk. paper)
1. Castles—Juvenile literature. 2. Civilization, Medieval—Juvenile literature. 3. Knights and knighthood—Juvenile literature. 4. Europe—Social life and customs—Juvenile literature. I. Title. II. Series.
GT3550 .G74 2003
J 940 .1—~~dc21~~
GRE

2002008114

Printed in China

Contents

CHAPTER ONE

Noble Strongholds

L ooming above valleys, defending mountain passes, protecting waterways—the ruins of thousands of castles guard the European countryside. Most castles were built during what historians call the Middle Ages, or medieval times.

During this period, from about 500 to 1500, powerful lords ruled hundreds of small kingdoms in Europe. They often fought with one another over land, power, and family honor. It was a violent, dangerous time.

To defend their lands and families from frequent attacks, great lords built fortresses called castles. By the end of the Middle Ages in the late fifteenth century, more than fifteen thousand castles stood watch across Europe.

At Home

Early castles were simple—a wooden or stone tower, called a donjon, or keep, was surrounded by a bailey (courtyard) and enclosed by thick walls. By the thirteenth century, castles were more elaborate. Various buildings—from keep to kitchen—stood behind the towering walls.

The Great Hall

The great hall was the center of castle life. Here lords and ladies conducted business, ate meals, entertained guests, and sometimes even slept.

The hall's large main room had tall walls, usually whitewashed, wood-paneled, or painted with colorful murals. Mounted on the walls were glittering weapons and hunting trophies—antlers, tusks, and animal heads. Bright **tapestries** hung about and blocked drafts.

Floors of beaten earth, stone, tile, or wood were laid with mats woven from grasses, flowers, and herbs. These

A lakeside castle, now in ruins, once protected Scottish lords from English attack.

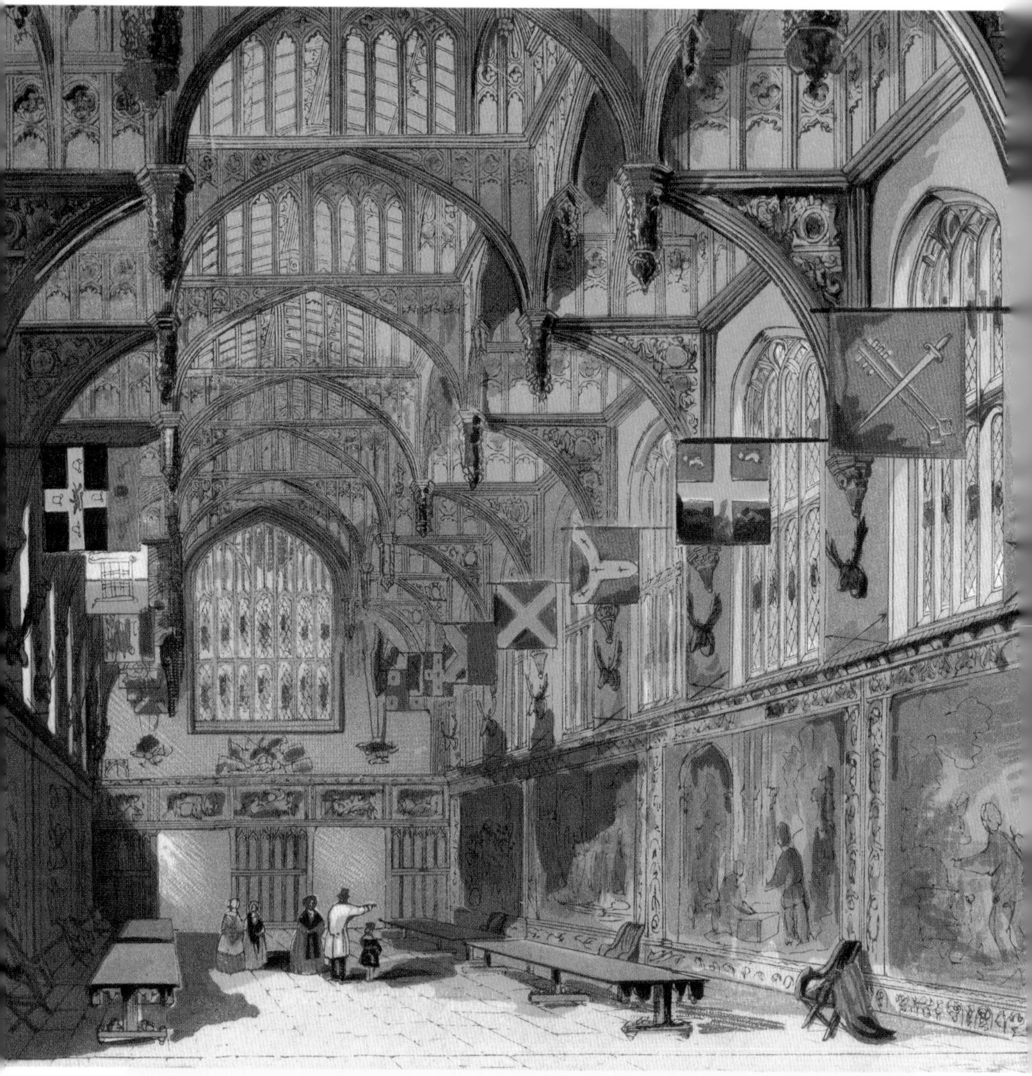

The great hall of a castle served as a place of business and entertainment.

sweet-smelling carpets protected against the chill and also helped hide the stench of dropped food and bones from mealtimes.

The hall's lower windows were narrow with heavy iron grills and wooden shutters for defense. The hall's upper windows were often large with small glass panes set in lead. At night or on dark winter days, light came from glowing candles, oil lamps, and torches. From the twelfth century on, huge fireplaces provided heat.

Furniture was limited and included wooden tables, storage chests, and an open cupboard for tableware. Benches, stools, and a few chairs provided seating. In early castles, the lord's high, curtained bed—the finest piece of furniture in the house—stood at one end of the hall screened by a wooden partition. Later the solar, an apartment on an upper story, provided a private living room and bedroom for the lord and lady.

Built into a small alcove nearby was a garderobe (toilet)—a simple raised stone platform with a hole in it that emptied into the watery moat or a pit. Torn strips of linen, unwanted letters, or a handful of scratchy straw were used as toilet paper.

The Chapel

Religion was an important part of people's everyday lives in the Middle Ages. Before the day began in the great hall, the lord and lady heard mass and prayed in the chapel. Most castles had a chapel. Many had more than one—a small, private one for the lord's family and a church-sized one for the rest of the castle community.

Whatever its size, the chapel was usually the most beautiful part of the castle. It was richly decorated with carved stone or woodwork, statues of saints, and stained glass windows. Colorful wall paintings showed stories from the Bible. A golden cross hung on the altar. A grand chapel showed the lord's great piety and wealth.

Nobles gather outside a church-sized chapel inside the castle walls.

Mealtimes and Manners

After chapel the lord and lady had a simple breakfast of bread and wine or ale. Dinner, the main meal of the day, was served between 10 A.M. and noon. A light meal, called supper, was served at dusk.

Dinner was a festive social event attended by the entire household. The lord's table was set on a raised platform at one end of the great hall. The rest of the tables were set at an angle. Thronelike chairs were reserved for the lord, lady, and honored guests. Everyone else sat on benches.

Diners, attended by servants armed with pitchers, basins, and towels, carefully washed their hands. After a blessing by the **chaplain**, a procession of servants brought in messes (platters and bowls) of food. Two diners shared each mess, heaping their individual portions onto thick, stale slices of bread called trenchers. Spoons were provided for soups, but diners used their fingers or the knives they carried at their waists for most dishes. Cups, like messes, were also shared.

With food and tableware shared and diners' fingers used as utensils, good manners were especially important. Courtesy books advised diners on polite behavior:

> Look thy hands be washed clean,
> That no filth on thy nails be seen . . .
> Pick not thine ears nor thine nostrils . . .
> Pick not thy teeth with thy knife . . .
> Spit thou not over the table, nor thereupon . . .
> Blow neither in thy meat or drink . . .[1]

A lord and his guests gather before a meal for the chaplain's blessing.

The Menu

Nobles ate well. Bread was eaten and wine or ale was drunk at every meal. Even an everyday dinner had three courses, each with several dishes from which to choose. Meat dishes—pork, beef, and mutton (sheep) from the lord's **manor**—were most often on the menu. A successful hunt provided game animals—deer, wild boar, and bear. Birds of all kinds—chicken, goose, and duck—and even storks, crows, seagulls, and eagles, were eaten. A variety of fish, often from the castle fishpond, were served on church fasting days when meat was not allowed. The orchard provided fruits, such as apples, pears, and plums. Garden vegetables included peas, beans, and onions.

The busy castle cook prepared these ingredients in many ways. Meats, poultry, and fish were regularly roasted, stewed, or made into pasties (pies). Or they might be pounded to a paste, mixed with other ingredients, and served as a kind of custard, called "blankmanger," or "mortrews," a kind of dumpling. Fruits were made into fancy tarts, fritters, and puddings. Vegetables were added to soups and stews or boiled with grains to make pottage (porridge).

Food was heavily spiced and served with rich sauces. Green sauce, made from herbs and wine, was frequently served with fish. Frumenty, made from wheat boiled in milk and spices, was delicious with beaver tail. Mustard sauce was served with everything from meat and fish to fruits, vegetables, and puddings. Chefs often tinted foods in rainbow colors with plant dyes, animal blood, or charcoal, and then they decorated them with sugared flowers and nuts.

A Medieval Feast

On special occasions, such as holidays and weddings, a splendid feast was held. A grand banquet impressed the lord's guests with his wealth and power.

An unimaginable number of strange and spectacular dishes were offered. Lifelike cooked swans with gilded (gold-coated) beaks and feet floated on green pastry

Guests crowd around a table to feast on spectacular dishes at a grand banquet.

ponds. Peacocks were served complete with their glistening feathers. A "cockatrice"—the upper part of a cooked rooster sewn to the hind end of a roasted pig—was a special surprise. Small birds were placed in pre-baked pies. When the pies were cut, the birds sang. Jugglers or acrobats leaped out of enormous puddings. Fountains spouted spiced wine and fragrant rosewater. But the most elaborate dish was the subtlety—an edible statue of brightly colored **marzipan**. Subtleties were molded to look like almost anything—ships, castles, cathedrals, famous people, even fire-breathing dragons.

Besides the showy food, there was entertainment. Musicians entertained guests from a raised gallery. Later there would be dancing or a silent play performed by mummers.

Clothing

For such a grand occasion, the lord's squire and the lady's maid helped them dress in their finest clothes. For much of the Middle Ages, men and women wore similar clothing.

First came loose linen undergarments—braies (breeches) and a chemise (shirt) for the lord, and a long chemise for the lady. Both pulled on silk stockings held in place with garters. Next, the tunic, a long, shirtlike garment, was slipped over the head and fastened with a brooch. Over that fit a second shorter tunic, called a surcoat. A girdle or belt tied or buckled at the waist. A semicircular cape, called a mantle, was fastened at the neck with another brooch or a chain and completed the outfit.

Clothes were brightly colored—blues, yellows, reds, purples, and greens. Fabrics were rich, often trimmed or

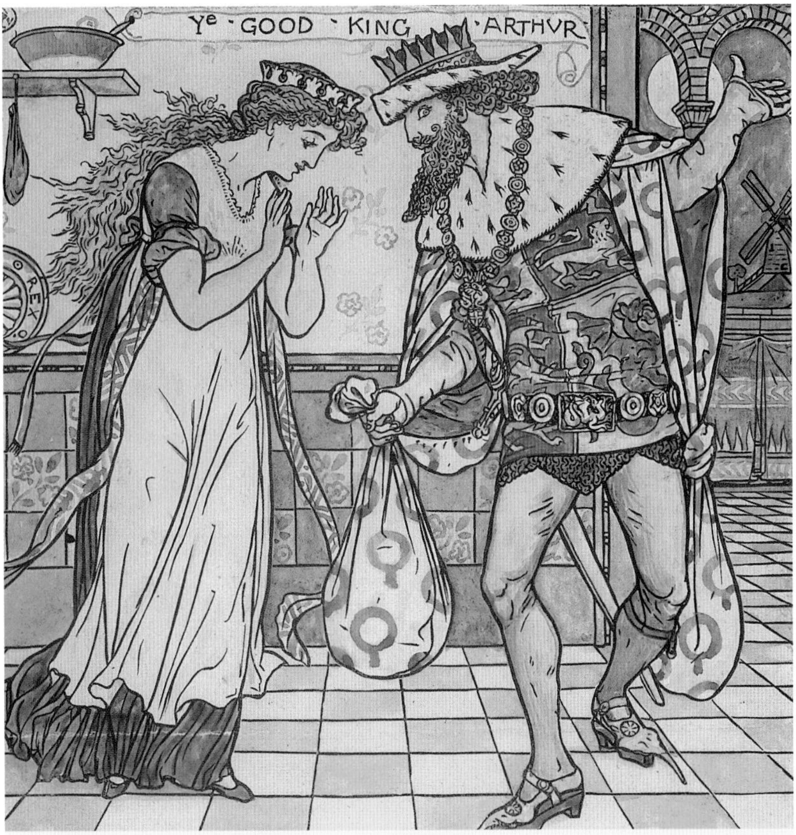
Ye · GOOD · KING · ARTHVR
REX

A lord and lady wear brightly colored and finely decorated clothes.

lined with fur, and decorated with embroidery, tassels, feathers, or beads. Belts and girdles might be made of gold or silver thread and studded with pearls or jewels.

For everyday wear, the lord and lady wore the same style clothing—tunic, surcoat, and mantle—but made of plain fabrics such as wool and cotton. These simpler clothes were more suitable for their daily activities as part of the castle community.

CHAPTER TWO

The Castle Community

I n the great hall the lord listens to his steward's report. His lady supervises the making of a fine tapestry in the solar. Several knights in the bailey cheer as their squires lunge at one another with dulled swords. Servants hurry about. The castle was a small, busy community.

The Lord

The lord ruled the castle and the lands it guarded. A lord was granted his land by the king or by another powerful nobleman, called his liege lord. In exchange for the land, or fief, the lord pledged his loyalty as a vassal (servant) to his liege. A solemn ceremony sealed the promise. The vassal knelt, placed both his hands between his liege lord's, and vowed, "Sir . . . I become your man . . . I swear and promise to . . . guard your rights with all my strength."[2] In turn, the liege lord promised to protect his vassal. This two-way promise was called the feudal bond.

The lord's most important duty to his liege was military service, usually about forty days a year. On the battlefield, he protected his liege with his own life—if necessary taking the liege's place as a prisoner. During peacetime, he guarded his liege's castle or acted as a bodyguard when his liege traveled. A lord was also obliged to help in his liege's courts and to entertain his liege as a guest in his castle. The lord also contributed toward large expenses, such as the knighting of his liege's eldest son, or ransoming his liege if he were captured.

Kneeling, a lord swears his allegiance to the king in a feudal bond.

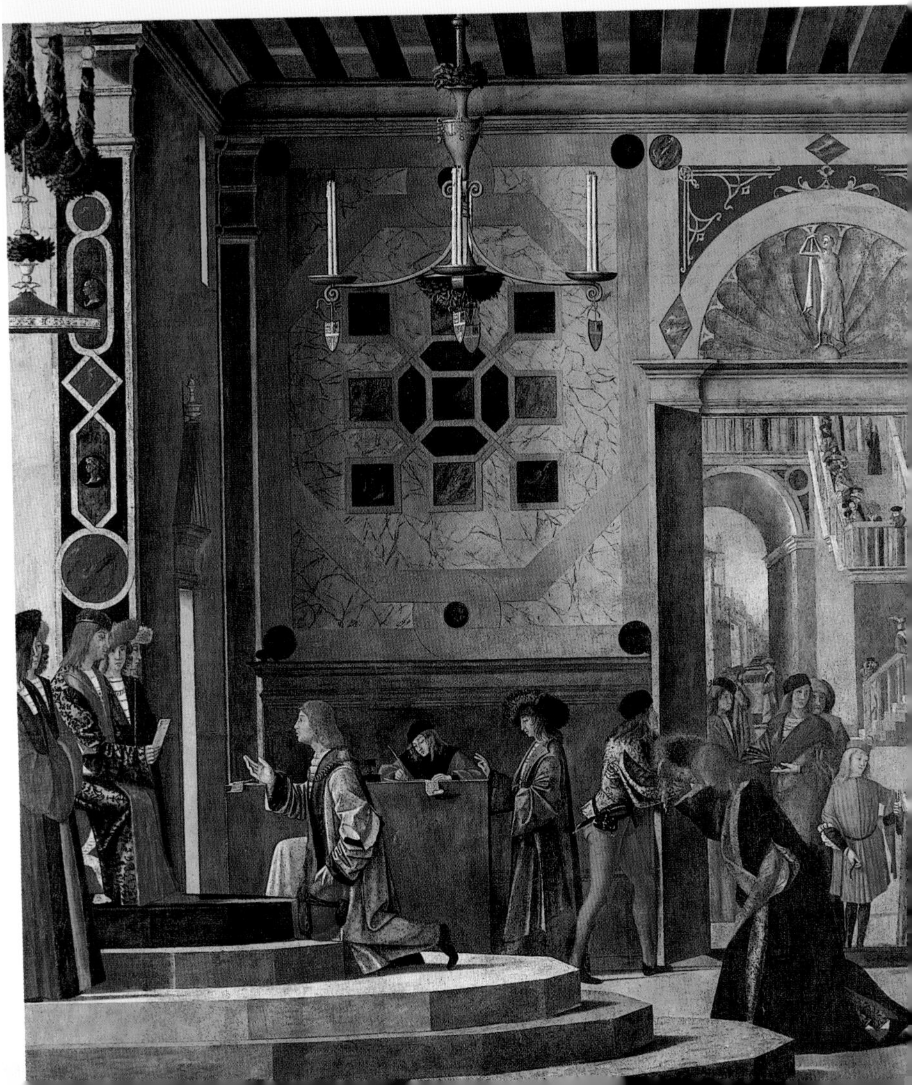

When he was not fulfilling his military duties, the lord was busy managing his fief. Land was wealth in the Middle Ages. An important lord often held several fiefs. His lands supplied him with farm products to use or sell. He also collected rents, taxes, and other fees from the tenants who lived on them. He held courts—settling quarrels and dispensing justice to his tenants and vassals of his own. A lord also frequently held a position in the royal government.

The Lady

While the lord managed and defended his lands, the lady ran the castle's daily routine. Whether the household had a dozen servants or hundreds, overseeing their work was her responsibility. She planned menus with the cook and supervised the spinsters' weaving of cloth and the tailors' making of clothes. She also directed a staff of workers from gardeners to grooms.

But busy as she was with household management, the lady's first duty was to give birth to sons to inherit the lord's fiefs. The lady usually had many children because few lived. Nursemaids provided much of the care. At the age of seven, noble sons and daughters were sent to the castle of a friend or relative to be educated.

While the lady sent her own children away, she, in turn, was usually responsible for the education of noble girls from other households. Her young charge, called a lady-in-waiting, learned social graces—to have good manners, dress fashionably, and be a gracious hostess— by observing the lady's behavior. Christine de Pisan, a famous author of the time, reminded noblewomen that "it

A lady and her servants entertain guests outside the castle.

is the duty of every princess and high-born lady . . . to excel in goodness, wisdom, manners, temperament, and conduct, so that she can serve as an example."[3] The lady would see to it that the girl also mastered fine needlework and learned to sing, dance, and play a musical instrument. She also made sure her student had lessons in basic mathematics, reading, languages, and religion from the castle chaplain. When the lady-in-waiting's training was complete, the lady's accomplished pupil would be ready to marry and run her own household.

A lady's education prepared her to be an important, though not equal, partner to her lord. Besides her role as manager, mother, and teacher, she was usually a skilled nurse—able to set bones broken in a tournament or prescribe an herbal remedy for a fever. She was also an expert hostess—entertaining powerful officials and guests. Finally, she might even defend the castle in the lord's absence. One grateful nobleman described his late wife as, "both fair and good, who had knowledge of all honor . . . and of fair behavior, and of all good she was the bell and flower."[4]

Knights

While his sister served as a lady-in-waiting learning to become a wife, a young nobleman trained to become a warrior, or knight. Becoming a knight required a long **apprenticeship**. It began when the boy was sent to the castle of a relative or friend to work as a page.

A young page spent much of his time with the lady and her attendants. He ran errands and helped with household chores—learning good manners as he served. He also practiced reciting poetry, singing, dancing, and perhaps playing a musical instrument. The castle chaplain provided his schooling and religious instruction. As he grew older, the castle's lord or one of his knights supervised his training in horsemanship, hunting, and fighting. Hearing stories and songs of famous heroes of the past, he learned to be brave and honorable. At about fourteen years of age, if the page had learned his lessons well, he became a squire.

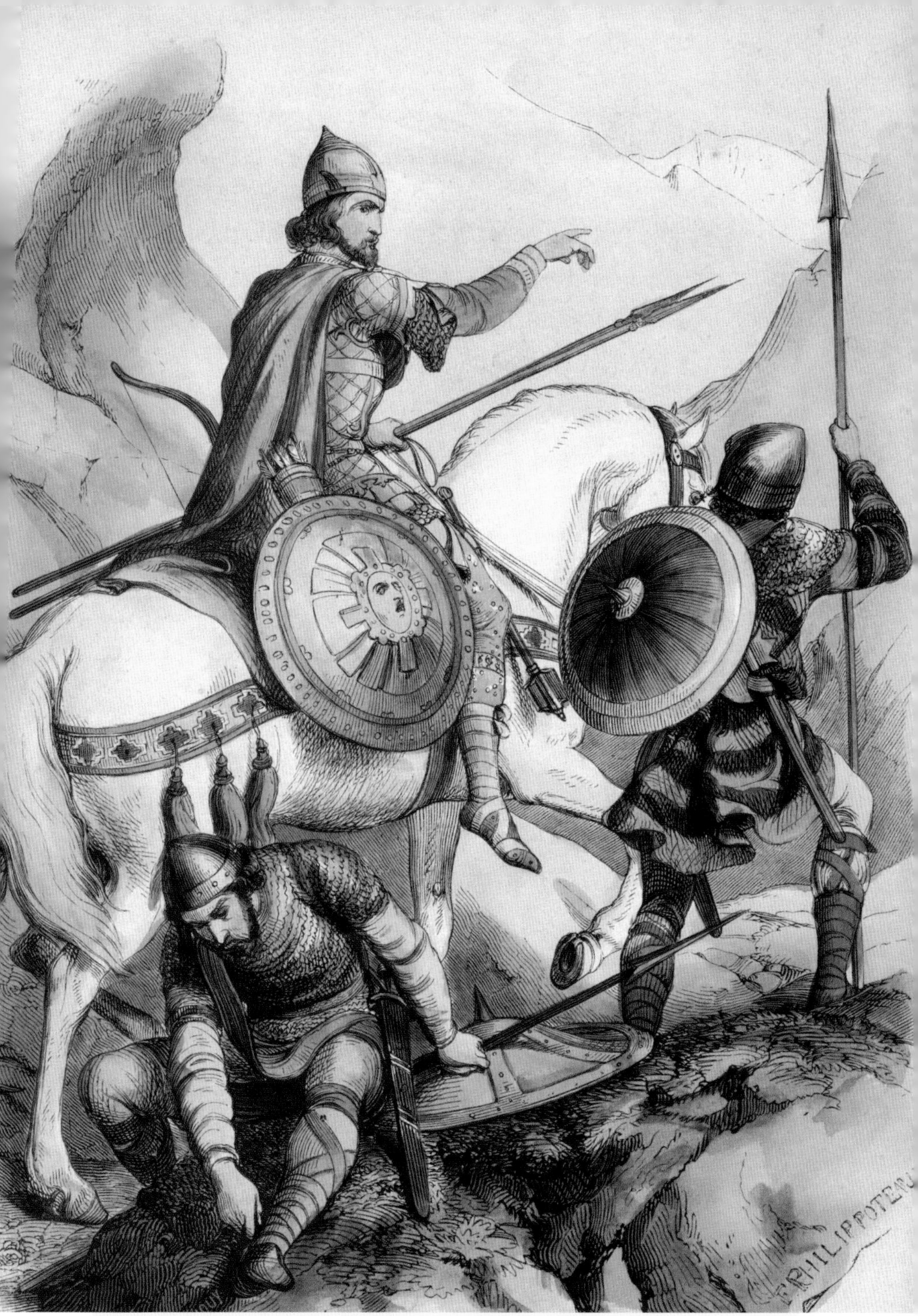

A knight supervises two apprentices in physical endurance training.

The squire was a true knight-in-training, acting as the companion and servant of a particular knight. He cared for his master's war horse, cleaned his master's armor, dressed and undressed him, and served him at meals. Most important, he prepared for war. Running races and wrestling with other squires made him strong. So did practicing for hours with heavy weapons, such as the sword, **mace**, and lance. An experienced squire also helped his master in tournaments. Eventually, he followed his master into battle, where he might—for exceptional bravery—become a knight himself.

But most squires were dubbed—declared knights—in a special ceremony at about age twenty-one. On the night before, the squire bathed and dressed in new clothing. He prayed and fasted alone in a church. In the morning, he knelt before his master, received a tap on the shoulder or neck with the flat side of a sword, and was presented with a sword and golden spurs.

Now he was also responsible for upholding the ideals of chivalry, the unwritten code of conduct by which a nobleman was expected to live. He was supposed to be brave and honorable, to protect the weak, and to respect women. Few knights always lived up to these high standards. Most treated other nobles well. But they often treated lowly servants and peasants harshly.

Household Servants

The number of servants employed in the castle depended on the lord's wealth. The **steward**, a kind of castle general manager, was the most important member of the lord's staff. Other key members of the lord's staff included the

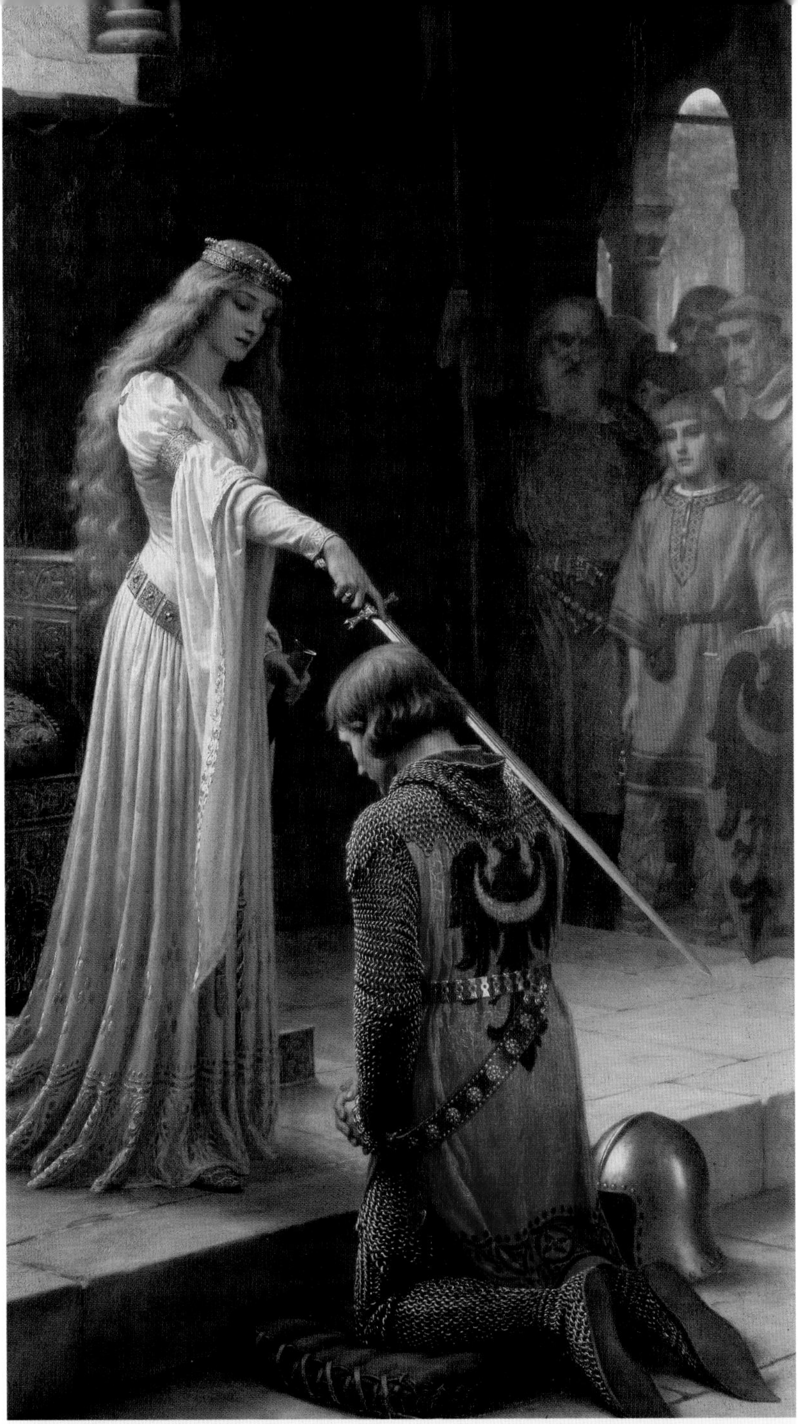

In the knighting ceremony a squire kneels before the princess who then touches his shoulder with a sword.

chaplain, treasurer, and cook. The stable marshal supervised the care of the lord's horses, hounds, and falcons.

Besides these high-ranking assistants, an army of others served. Some had special skills, such as the carpenter and the blacksmith. Others were craftsmen—such as soap and candle makers. Most were lowly menials—unskilled laborers such as watchmen, porters, and kitchen help.

Most servants were unmarried men. A few, such as the laundress who washed the clothes, sheets, towels, and tablecloths, were women.

The Peasants

The lives of everyone inside the castle, from lord to laundress, depended on the work of the peasants, or farmers, who lived outside its walls. About 90 percent of the population was made up of peasants. Most peasants were serfs, unable to leave the land without the lord's permission. Serfs lived in villages on their lord's manor, planting and harvesting his crops and caring for his livestock. If required, serfs also served in the lord's army.

In return, serfs were given small plots of land on which to raise food for their families. The lord promised to protect them, and they could seek refuge inside the castle walls during wartime. A serf's life was hard and often cut short by starvation, disease, or war.

Not All Work and Warfare

Maintaining and protecting a great castle was a challenge. But important lords had a staff of busy servants

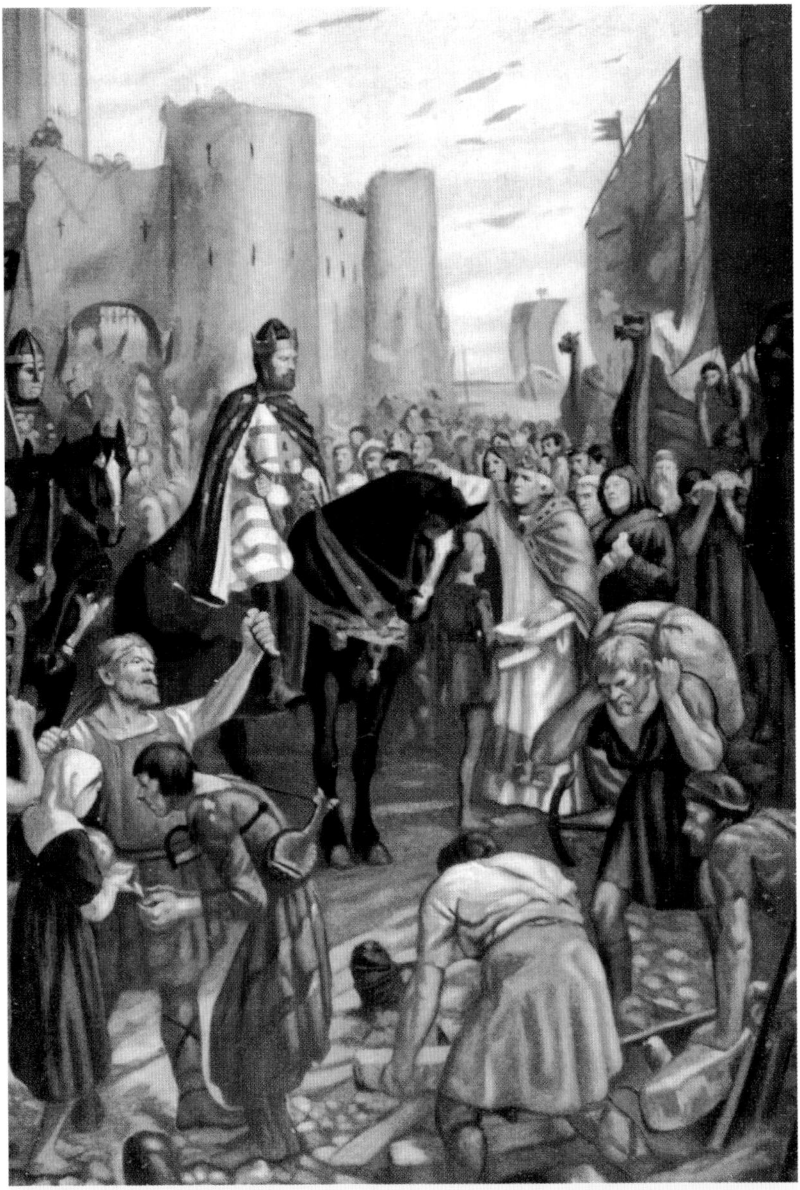

Peasants and serfs carry goods to the king and his guards.

and an army of battle-ready knights and reluctant peasants for the task. This gave the lord and his family time to enjoy a variety of amusements.

CHAPTER THREE

Amusements

I n peacetime, lords and ladies entertained themselves with many pastimes. But even when no invaders threatened, nobles still found ways to pursue the danger and drama of war.

The Hunt

The thrill of the chase and kill made hunting the most popular pastime for medieval lords. Because hunting required skill with weapons, horsemanship, and strategy, it was good practice for war, too.

A successful hunt also meant fresh meat for the lord's dinner table. Many kinds of animals, from foxes and wolves to deer and bear, were hunted. But the razor-sharp tusks of the wild boar made it the fiercest kill. Writing in 1410, Edward, duke of York, warned, "The boar slayeth a man with one stroke, as with a knife. Some have seen him slit a man from knee up to breast, and slay him all stark dead with one stroke."[5]

Despite the dangers, a hunt was a festive occasion. The hunting party rode into the forest early. While they

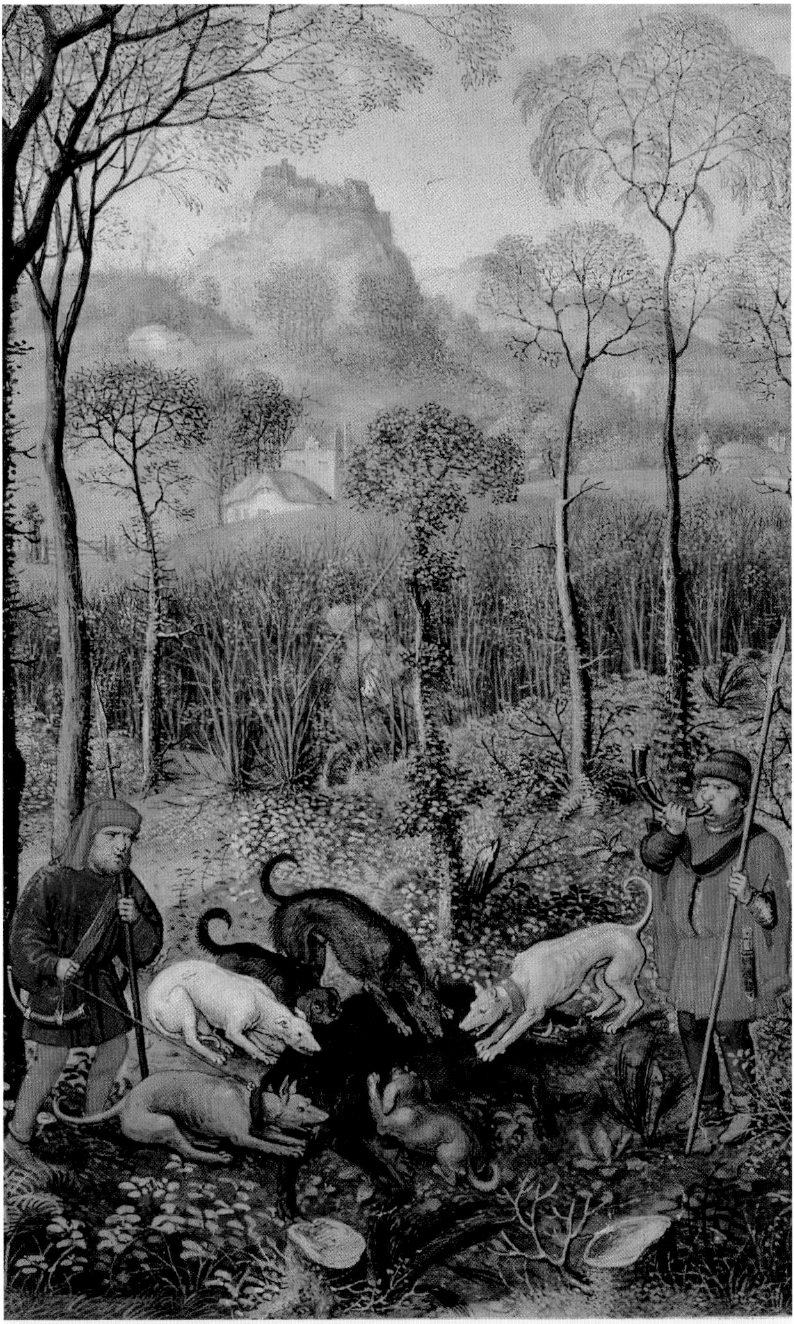

A huntsman blows a horn to signal others in his party that the dogs have captured a boar.

enjoyed a picnic breakfast, the lord's huntsman stalked the animals with dogs.

When signs of prey, such as a deer's tracks, were discovered, the huntsman examined them and tried to guess the animal's size and age. Then he would collect some of its droppings to show the lord. If the lord decided the animal was worthy game, the huntsman and dogs quietly set off to block the deer's retreat.

Armed with spears and bows, the eager hunting party waited. When the lord blew his ivory hunting horn, the chase began. The dogs leaped after the deer, and the nobles followed. When the dogs finally cornered the animal, one of the noblemen was given the honor of killing it. Afterward, the animal was skinned and the meat divided. The hardworking dogs received a generous share.

Nobles took their hunting fun seriously. They set aside large areas of their land as private game preserves. Strict forest laws forbid peasants to hunt there. A **poacher** caught with so much as a rabbit faced harsh punishment—being blinded, or even killed.

Birds with Brains

Falconry, using birds of prey to hunt small animals and other birds, was the most popular kind of hunting. Although pursuing large, dangerous game animals was mainly a sport for noblemen, falconry—often called hawking—was a favorite of both lord and lady.

Most nobles owned birds. The kind of bird they hunted with depended on their place in society. Keeping a bird above your rank was punishable by having your hands cut off.

Hunting birds were expensive to train and keep. Young birds were captured and housed in a special building called a mews. Fierce and temperamental, a bird needed patient training by the lord's falconer.

The bird was readied for training by having its eyes temporarily sewn closed. Its first lesson was learning to ride on its master's glove-protected wrist. The thirteenth-century work, *The Art of Hunting with Birds,* instructs falconers that the bird "be gently carried round in a dark room, alone with her keeper. This must go on for a day and a night."[6] As the bird became familiar with its new life, the stitches were loosened and its sight restored. Then, using a lure made from the meat-baited wings of

Two men, holding their falcons, await the start of the hunt.

its intended prey, the bird was taught to return to its master during the hunt. Finally, the bird was taught to pursue its prey—often practicing on live game—such as a crane whose beak was bound and whose claws were blunted.

A favorite bird might share its master's bedroom and sit on the back of his chair at meals. One thirteenth-century king, Frederick II of Hohenstaufen, loved falconry so much that he lost an important military campaign when he went hawking instead of continuing to besiege a fortress!

Tournaments and Jousts

Hunting and hawking were challenging peacetime amusements. But many noblemen missed the battlefield because they were afraid of losing their fighting skills.

War games, called tournaments, began as military training. Roger de Hoveden, a twelfth-century writer, claimed "a knight cannot shine in war if he has not prepared for it in tournaments. He must have seen his own blood flow, have had his teeth crackle under the blow of an adversary. . . . Then he will be able to confront actual war with the hope of being victorious."[7]

Early tournaments were wild, violent brawls without rules or referees. Small armies of mounted knights met on a field. At a signal, they charged one another. A romance of the time describes the confusing scene: "Lances break and shields are riddled, the hauberks [armor] receive bumps and are torn asunder, saddles go empty and horsemen tumble, while the horses sweat and foam."[8] Prisoners were taken for ransom, and their horses and ar-

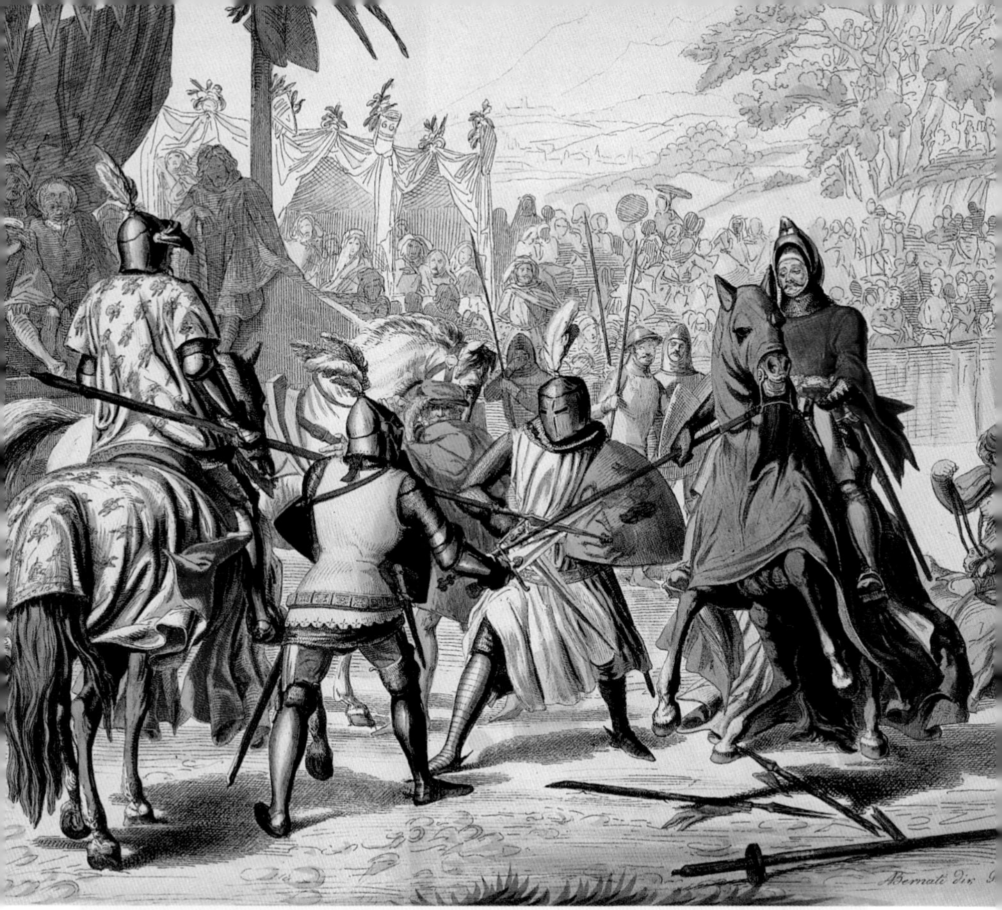

Dueling on foot, two knights fight for honor in a tournament.

mor claimed as spoils of war. Called a melee or fracas, these games were often fatal. At a tournament given at Neuss in 1241, more than eighty knights died.

Gradually, these deadly contests gave way to tournaments resembling pageants given to celebrate an important occasion. **Heralds** rode through the countryside inviting knights to compete. An arena, called the lists, was built. Viewing stands were carpeted and hung with tapestries and banners. The stands sheltered the finely dressed lords and ladies there to cheer for their favorite knights. The tournaments included wrestling matches, lance- and

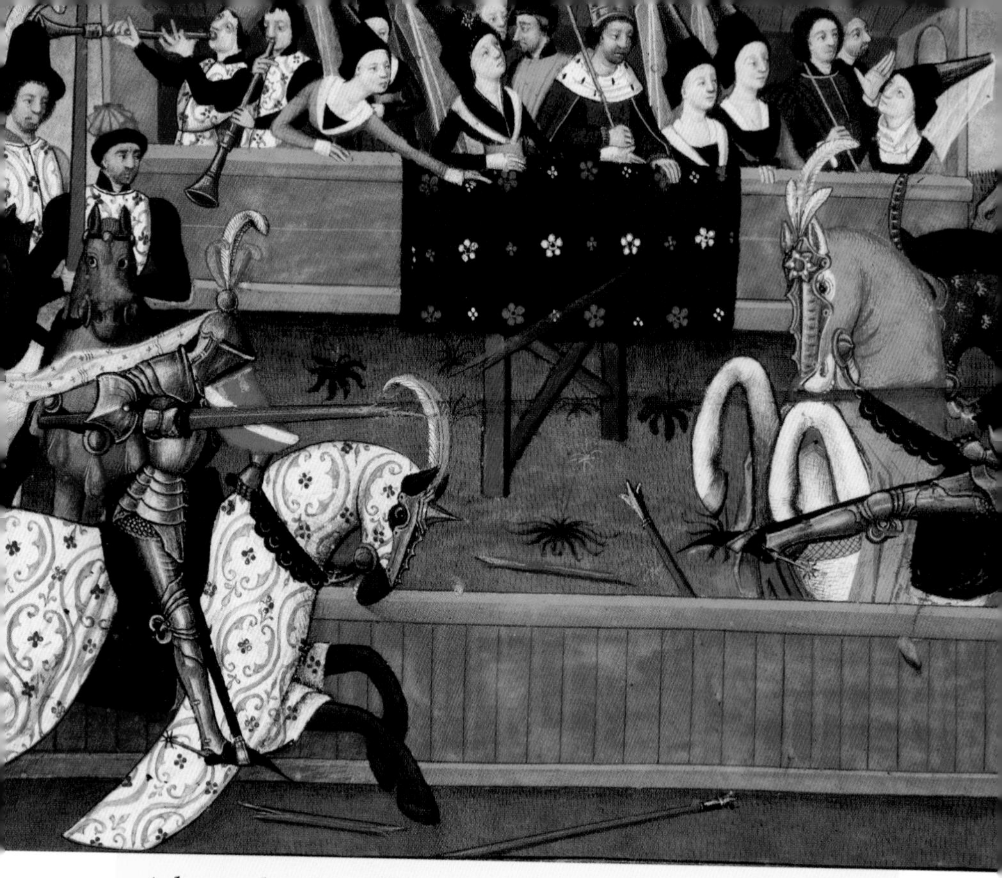

A horse bucks off its master after he was struck by his opponent's lance.

stone-throwing contests, and sometimes a well-ordered melee. But the most popular event was the joust—a duel on horseback.

Jousting knights faced one another at opposite ends of the lists. Then, with lowered lances, they galloped hard toward one another, each trying to knock the other from his horse. Points were scored for unhorsing an opponent, for breaking his lance, and for knocking off his helmet. If a knight lost his lance, he fought on with a sword, battle-ax, or mace. The joust could last for days. The winners of each joust fought one another for the admiration of the crowd and the rich prizes—a diamond brooch or a golden shield—given by their host. Though contestants wore heavy armor and used blunted weapons, injuries, even deaths, were common.

Making Merry

Not all medieval merriment was murderous. Nobles enjoyed lively performances by entertainers from musicians and storytellers to jugglers and **jesters**. Traveling

Four men play a game of tables.

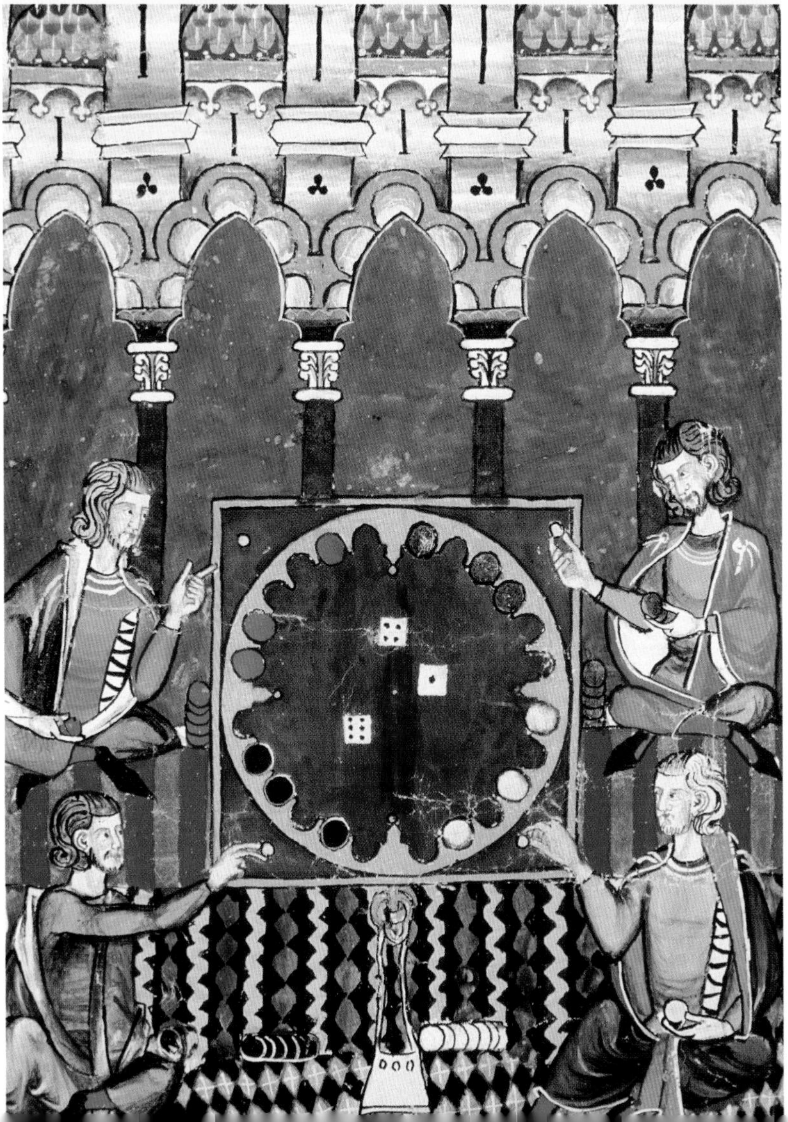

performers, such as acrobats, actors, and animal trainers, were also welcomed. Board games, including chess, tables (backgammon), and merels (a tic-tac-toe-type game), were played on cold winter days. Dancing and active games such as hoodman's blind, a kind of tag, were popular, too. But while nobles had many amusements, their main pastime was making war.

CHAPTER FOUR

The Castle at War

W ar was a fact of life in the Middle Ages. Most battles were centered around castles. An enemy seeking to conquer an area plotted against the castles protecting it. Whoever held the castles controlled the land. As the stronghold of a noble's power, a castle was built to defend against enemy attack.

High on a Hill

The first line of defense was a castle's location. Most castles were built atop rocky cliffs or steep hillsides. High locations were hard for a heavily armed enemy to climb. Perched above the surrounding countryside, alert lookouts were also able to watch for invaders.

Another favorite spot was near water—along a coast, on an island, or near a lake or river. Locating a castle here provided it with a natural moat or with water to fill a man-made one. A moat was an important defense. It was spanned by a drawbridge, which the guards could raise, cutting off entry to the castle. Attackers trying to swim across the moat risked drowning

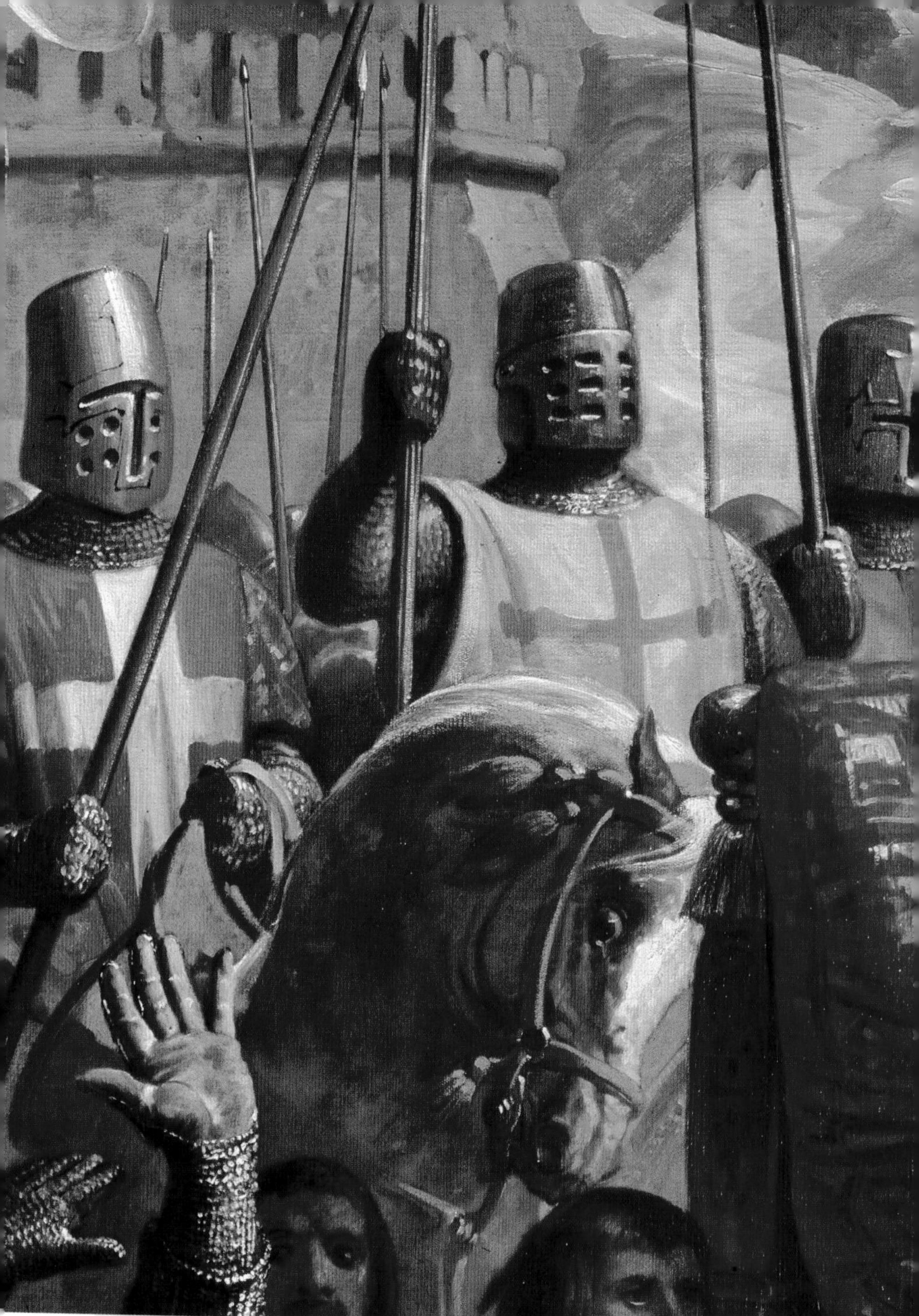

Heavily armored knights prepare to defend the castle high on the hill behind them.

and made easy targets for the expert archers on the walls. Even if a moat were left dry, its steep sides made it difficult to cross. Sharpened sticks planted in the moat added to the danger.

Walled Off

Beyond the moat loomed the castle walls. By the twelfth century, one or more stone **curtain walls** encircled the castle. If the enemy got through the first wall, they still had to fight their way through the second. Often the inner wall was built higher than the outer wall. This allowed archers on the inner wall to shoot at the attackers above the defenders stationed on the outer wall.

Curtain walls could be thirty to more than forty feet high and seven to twenty feet thick. At the top were **battlements** with toothlike gaps, called crenels, through which hidden soldiers would fire on the enemy. Galleries of wood, called hoardings, or of stone, called machicolations, often projected from the battlements. Through floor openings, unwary attackers were bombarded with stones or had boiling liquids dropped on their heads.

Great towers jutted from strategic points along the wall. These strengthened the walls, added space to store provisions against a siege, and housed the **garrison**. Arrow loops provided archers with a wide field of fire against advancing attackers. Nicknamed "murderesses," these loops were slitlike on the outside and flared on the inside to help guide the defenders' arrows on their deadly paths.

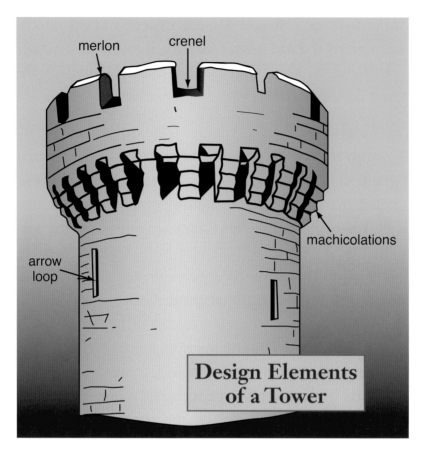

merlon

crenel

machicolations

arrow loop

Design Elements of a Tower

Enemy at the Gate

A massive gatehouse stood at the castle's entrance, a likely point of attack. Some castles also had a barbican, or extra gatehouse, extending from the castle walls and protecting the main gatehouse.

Flanked by two huge towers with guardrooms, an **armory**, and space for a prison, the gatehouse was equipped with one or more portcullises. These grilled doors, spiked on the bottom and plated with iron, slid down to block the heavy wooden gatehouse door. If attackers succeeded in breaking through, they still had to pass under "murder holes." These were gaps in the ceiling above the entrance passage where soldiers rained rocks, scalding liquids, and hot sand down on them.

Keep Out!

Fighting their way across the bailey, invaders faced the keep. Built as the lord's last refuge and the castle's command post during a siege, a keep might be surrounded by its own wall, moat, and drawbridge. Some keeps were more than eighty feet high and had walls seventeen feet thick. A staircase, protected in its own building, was the only way to

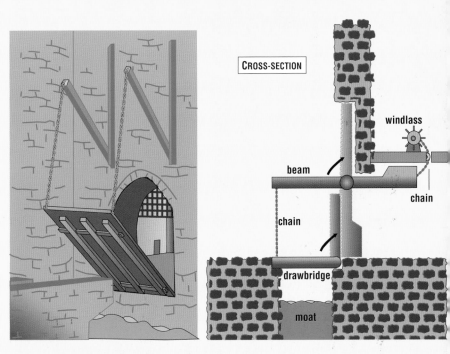

A Counterweight Drawbridge

CROSS-SECTION

windlass

beam

chain

chain

drawbridge

moat

Some castle drawbridges operated by means of counterweights. The wooden drawbridge normally rested over the moat. To raise the bridge, defenders allowed the heavy rear ends of large beams to fall. As the lighter front ends rose, they raised the bridge by means of chains connecting the two.

reach the stronghold's remote second- or third-story entrance. Inside, a wall often divided the keep in half with a way through the system of passages and staircases known only by the occupants. A rear sally port gave a fleeing lord an escape route. Well-stocked basement storage rooms and

Tourists visit a castle keep, a protected building that served as the lord's stronghold during attacks.

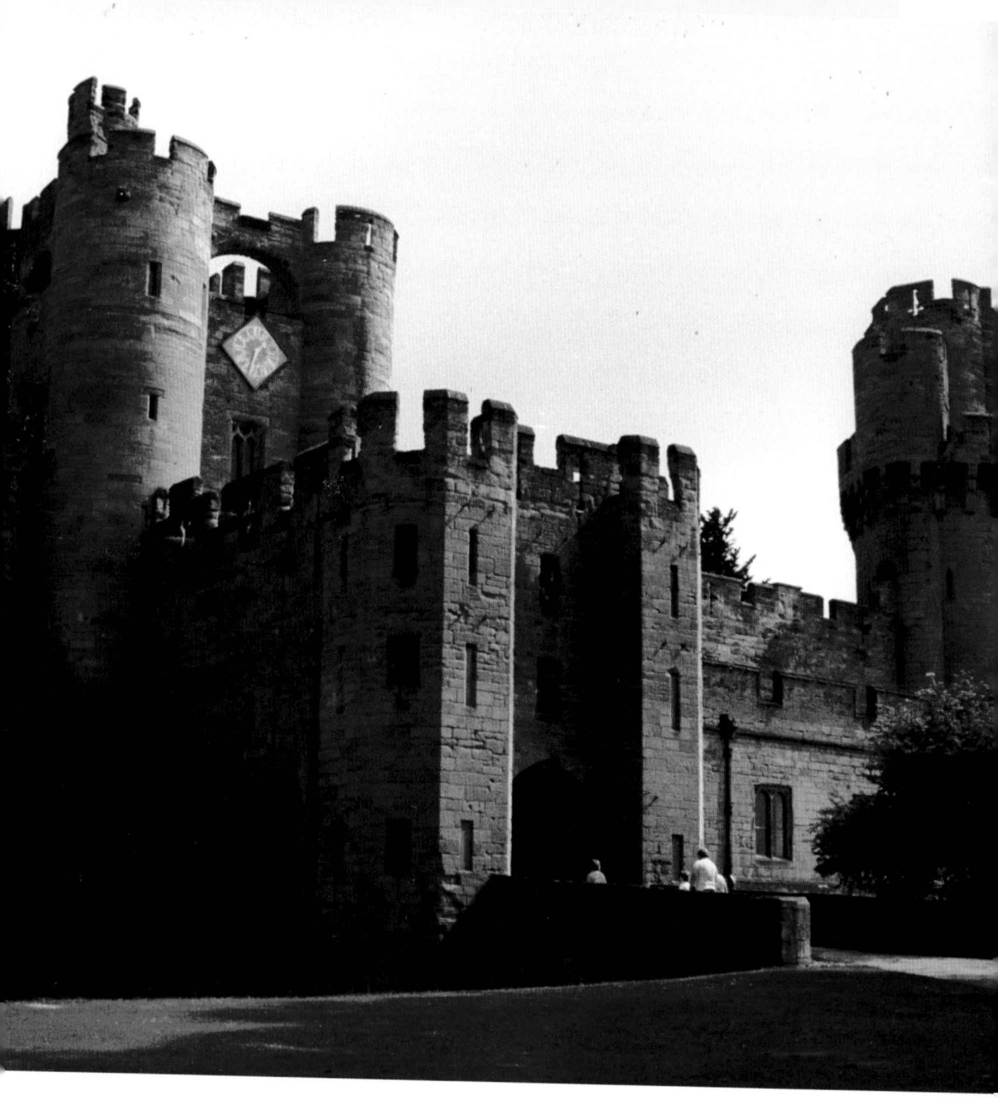

an indoor well made the keep self-sufficient. Despite these precautions, once the castle's walls were breached, this fortress would usually fall to its attackers.

To Fight or Not to Fight?

But breaching a castle's walls was a long and costly ordeal. Before risking this step, a clever invader often tried other schemes.

Quietly scaling the walls at night to capture the sleeping garrison was an effective plan. So was having a small party of knights create a diversion while another group attacked. Scouts studying the castle grounds might find a secret way in—through a garbage chute, dried-up well, even a smelly latrine pipe—and launch a surprise attack.

Trickery was also popular. A few soldiers disguised as peasants or hidden in a grain-filled wagon might be smuggled into the castle in advance. When the attack came, they opened the gate for their comrades. A sly invader might forge surrender instructions from an absent lord or bribe a household member.

The Siege

If these plots failed, hostile troops lay siege to the castle—surrounding it and stopping anyone from leaving and preventing supplies from getting in. But a well-stocked castle could last for months, so the commander made plans to take it by force.

Undermining was one way to topple the castle's walls. Miners slowly dug under the walls, supporting their tunnel with wooden beams. Then they filled it

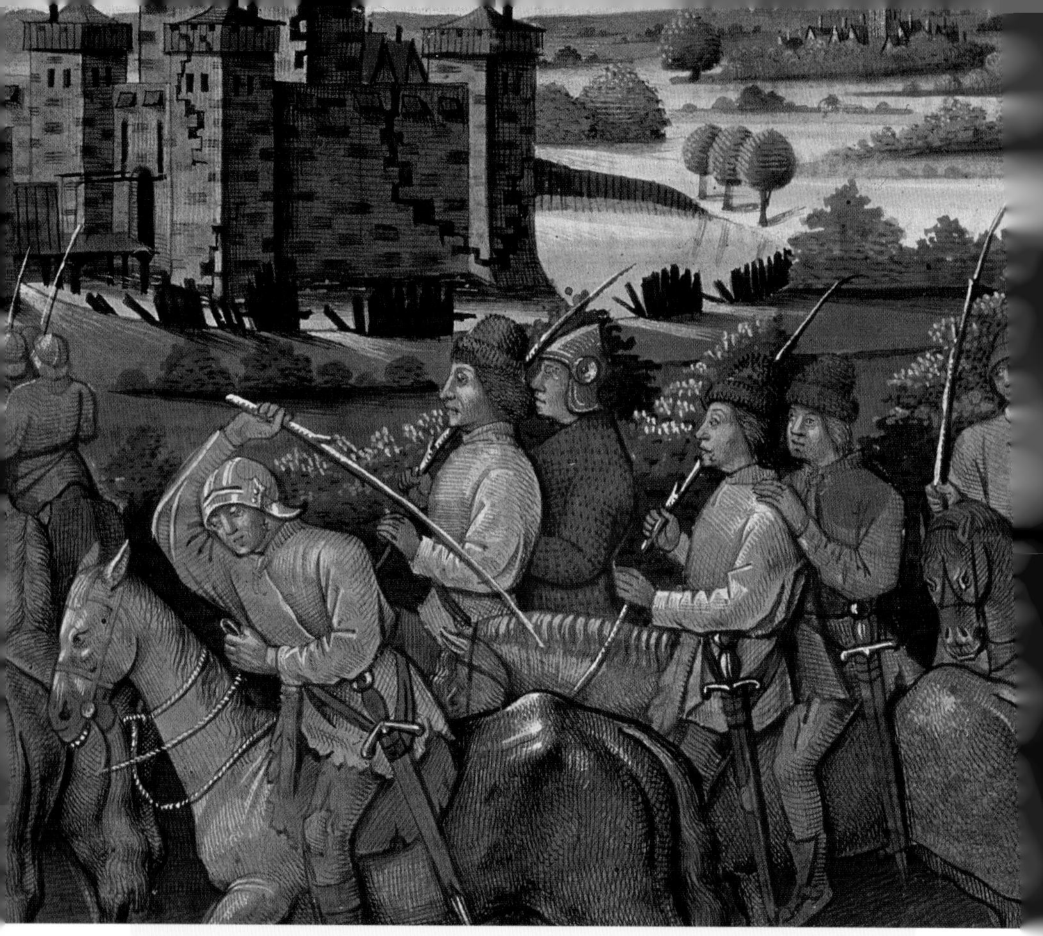

Foot soldiers and horsemen surround a castle, preventing people and supplies from getting in or out.

with a flammable material—straw, brush, even pig **carcasses**—and set it on fire. When the beams burned away, the tunnel and the wall above it collapsed.

Various siege engines were also used. Stone throwers could catapult fifty-pound rocks a distance of two hundred yards. But the trebuchet was even more terrible. This engine could hurl ammunition weighing several hundred pounds as far as a quarter of a mile! Attackers also used it to launch disease-spreading dead animals, dung, or the heads of hostages into the castle. Even worse was "Greek fire." This flaming mixture, packed into clay pots that shattered on impact, stuck to whatever it hit and could not be put out with water. A thirteenth-century knight wrote: "This Greek fire was like a large barrel, and its tail was the length of a long spear; the noise which it made was like thunder, and it seemed a great dragon of fire flying through the air."[9]

Soldiers attack a castle, setting it ablaze.

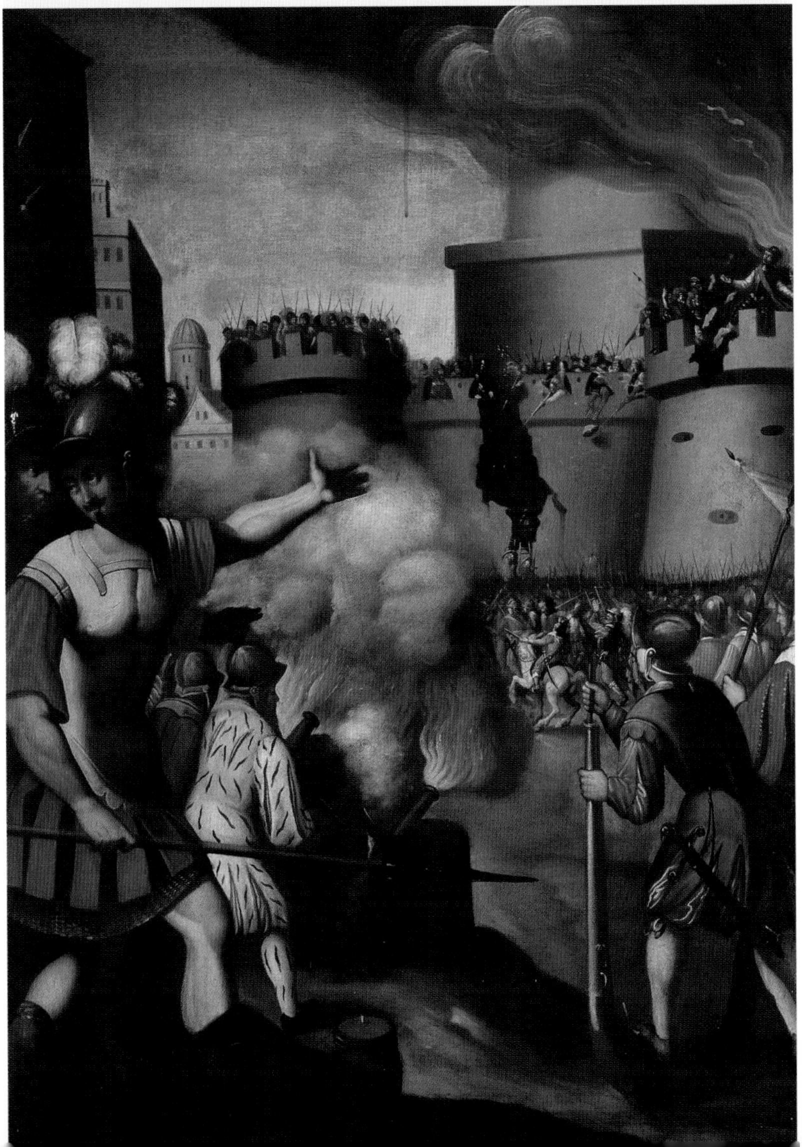

The enemy might scale the walls using a tower or belfry. Looming above the castle walls, it consisted of several floors, shielded by wooden sides and draped in wet animal hides against fiery missiles. Troops, hidden beneath wheeled shelters called "cats" or "tortoises," first filled the moat, then pushed the belfry up to the walls. A drawbridge was lowered, and the soldiers hidden inside charged across the battlements.

Other weapons included the ballista, a giant crossbow whose arrows could skewer several soldiers at once, and the battering ram, a heavy tree trunk used to pound in the gatehouse door or even the curtain wall.

Hunger and Thirst

Many castles held off these attacks. But as supplies ran low, disease and starvation spread. The besieged ate anything they could find—rats, grass, and boiled saddle leather. They drank their livestock's blood, even one another's urine.

If the desperate besieged surrendered, they were often allowed to retreat unharmed. If the castle were taken by force, its occupants were frequently slaughtered. Fourteenth-century historian Jean Froissart described the brutal end of the siege of Limoges: "It was a great pity to see the men, women, and children that kneeled before the prince for mercy . . . more than 3,000 . . . were slain and beheaded that day."[10]

Sometimes, however, a lord's friends would rescue the castle, or the enemy would just give up and march off—defeated by the castle's determined defenders and its mighty walls.

Notes

Chapter One: Noble Strongholds

1. Quoted in Edith Rickert and L.J. Naylor, trans., *The Babees' Book: Medieval Manners for the Young.* www.yorku.ca.

Chapter Two: The Castle Community

2. Quoted in Jay Williams, *Life in the Middle Ages.* New York: Random House, 1966, p. 13.
3. Quoted in *Le Livere des Trois Vertus.* Medieval Women: An Interactive Exploration. www.mw.mcmaster.ca.
4. Quoted in Joseph and Frances Gies, *Life in a Medieval Castle.* New York: Harper & Row, 1974, p. 79.

Chapter Three: Amusements

5. Quoted in Gies, *Life in a Medieval Castle,* p. 126.
6. Quoted in Peter Speed, ed., *Those Who Fought: An Anthology of Medieval Sources.* New York: Ithaca Press, 1996, p. 119.
7. Quoted in Walter C. Meller, *A Knight's Life in the Days of Chivalry.* London: T. Werner Laurie Limited, 1924, p. 133.
8. Quoted in Maurice Keen, *Chivalry.* New Haven, CT: Yale University Press, 1984, p. 85.

Chapter Four: The Castle at War

9. Quoted in Williams, *Life in the Middle Ages,* p. 101.
10. Quoted in Speed, *Those Who Fought,* p. 103.

Glossary

apprenticeship: A period of training, usually under the direction of someone with that skill.

armory: A place where weapons are stored.

battlements: The top of a defending wall.

carcasses: The bodies of dead animals.

chaplain: A priest.

curtain walls: Outer castle walls enclosing a courtyard.

garrison: Soldiers stationed in a castle.

heralds: Messengers.

jesters: Court clowns.

mace: A metal club, often fitted with spikes or chains.

manor: A farm.

marzipan: Almond paste.

nobles: Men (and women) of the highest social class in medieval society.

poacher: A person who hunts illegally.

steward: The most important servant, often in charge of estate management.

tapestries: Woven or painted wall hangings.

For Further Exploration

Books

Christopher Gravett, *The World of the Medieval Knight*. New York: Peter Bedrick, 1996. Explores the world of the medieval knight including his education, castle life, and warfare.

Kathryn Hinds, *Life in the Middle Ages: The Castle*. New York: Benchmark Books, 2001. Period illustrations show how lords and ladies dressed, ate, and entertained.

Fiona MacDonald, *A Medieval Castle*. New York: Peter Bedrick, 1993. Clear cutaway illustrations and informative captions provide a detailed look at castle life.

Philip Steele, *Castles*. New York: Kingfisher, 1995. Colorful illustrations, including a four-page foldout section of a castle inside and out, provide information about how castles were built and how their inhabitants lived.

Websites

Castles of the World (www.castles.org). This site has photographs of castles from all over the world. It also includes a section for students with information about the people and parts of a castle.

Castles on the Web (www.castlesontheweb.com). This site has links to dozens of castles, information for students, a castle glossary, a picture archive, and more.

Medieval Women (www.mw.mcmaster.ca). This interactive site from McMaster University in Canada explores the medieval world through the eyes of women. Includes music, sound effects, and narration from the castle, convent, and farm.

Medieval World (www.geocities.com). This site has a gallery with images of medieval artwork, a library of articles about medieval life, and hundreds of links to other sites about the Middle Ages.

National Geographic Society (www.nationalgeographic.com). At this interactive site you can explore a "haunted" fourteenth-century castle—guided by the "ghosts" of its guards, jesters, squires, and other inhabitants who share what castle life was like.

Public Broadcasting System (www.pbs.org). A section of the site was developed as part of the *NOVA* television special "The Medieval Siege." Both offensive weapons and defensive strategies are illustrated and discussed.

Index